THE GOLDEN COYOTE

THE GOLDEN COYOTE

BY EILEEN THOMPSON

Illustrated by RICHARD CUFFARI

SIMON AND SCHUSTER   NEW YORK

To my mother and to the memory of my father,
Nelle and Hugh Thompson,
and to all those of all times
who love the Pajarito Plateau,
this book is affectionately dedicated.

Text copyright © 1971 by Eileen Thompson
Illustrations copyright © 1971 by Richard Cuffari
Published by Simon and Schuster, Children's Book Division
Rockefeller Center, 630 Fifth Avenue
New York, New York 10020
First printing
SBN 671-65193-5 Reinforced Edition
Library of Congress Catalog Card Number: 73-159530
Manufactured in the United States of America

CONTENTS

hELLO ANO FAREWELL

"Look, Little Otter! Coyote pups!"

Snow Feather began to run up the rocky talus slope toward the cliff wall. At the mouth of a small cave, a half-dozen furry tan pups were tumbling about in play.

"Wait!" Little Otter's tone of alarm halted the younger boy.

"What's the matter?"

"The mother and father, they must be close by. An angry mother coyote I would not want to face."

"You're right. I didn't think."

"Leaping Deer taught me that. Listen! Are those two coyotes barking up on the far mesa?"

"I think so."

"Then it should be safe to play with the pups for a few minutes, but just a few."

The boys scrambled up to the cave, one of many that pocked the soft volcanic rock of the cliff. Each scooped up a warm, wriggling animal. Snow Feather giggled as his pup, with an inquisitive nose, sniffed about under his chin, tickling him.

"Hello, small one," said Little Otter. "How I would like to have you for a pet!"

"You know we're not allowed to. Besides, why do you need a pet? You're lucky, Little Otter. You have Leaping Deer for your godfather. You do many things together. He teaches you so much. My godfather is too busy. Such a big family he has! He has to work all day long just to feed them. I'm the one who needs a pet, not you."

"Well, neither of us can have one, so there's no use talking about it. I wish Leaping Deer would get back. He's been gone for three days. I wanted him to take me with him when he went to hunt in the mountains. But the snows up there, he said, would be too deep for me. You are right. I am lucky. What a man he is! Because he is my godfather, everyone *has* to be nice to me, even if they don't want to—even if my mother isn't of our people."

"Don't be cross. *I* like you, anyway."

Little Otter had to laugh at the comical mixture of concern and mischief on Snow Feather's face. "I know. But sometimes . . ." He sighed and held his pup closer, stroking it gently. "This one is not as dark as the others. It is almost the color of honey."

The pup turned her head, looking up into the boy's black eyes—eyes that now reflected the troubled tone of his voice. "I don't understand. What does it matter where a person is born? My mother is a very good person. So what if she wasn't born here? My father is good too. And besides, he was born in the very room where we live now."

"I think it's silly. I guess it's because we don't get many strangers on this plateau. People don't like them just because they don't know them."

"You're probably right. But it's been so many years! After all, Snow Feather, I was born here, and I'm almost old enough now to be initiated into the secrets of the society of my father. Oh, there's no use talking about it."

Little Otter sat down in front of the coyote den. It was a tingling sunny day such as often follows a heavy snowfall in the early spring. For the first time in several full moons, the Indian boys were clad only in their loincloths, without their warm shoulder capes of rabbit skins. Here in the rock-warmed canyon, the snows of a few days before were already gone, evaporated by the dry Southwest air. On the high slopes of the western mountains, though, the sun gleamed on a blanket of icy whiteness that weighted down the forests of pine and spruce. Up there, the wind blew sharp as the edge of an obsidian knife, and the drifts in the ravines lay deep enough to cover a tall man. Little Otter shivered, suddenly frightened for no reason.

"What's wrong with that one's ear?" Snow Feather asked, recalling Little Otter from his thoughts.

The larger boy bent over the puppy in his arms, grateful for the diversion. Snow Feather was a good friend, even though he was a few years younger. Little Otter appreciated that friendship. Many of the boys in the village on the mesa followed the example of their parents and treated Little Otter and his mother, Blue Corn, with scarcely hidden antagonism.

"One of the other pups must have nipped it when they were playing. See? There's a little piece gone. It won't matter, though. It's already healed."

Little Otter lifted his head, listening intently. "What was that? Did you hear anything?"

As he spoke, he jumped to his feet and stepped away from the cliff wall, looking up the canyon. His heart thumped heavily. "It sounded like a call. There! Did you hear it? Someone's in trouble."

Snow Feather put down his coyote and joined him. "Yes. Was it from the trail, do you think?"

Little Otter also bent and carefully deposited his pup with the others. Then, as another call rang out, he started to run.

"It's Leaping Deer," he called back. "I see him. Go to the village for help! Hurry! Oh, Snow Feather, hurry!"

But even as he sped up the trail toward the weaving, lurching figure, he felt again the cold touch of fear.

Several full moons later, grief still burdened Little Otter like a great black bear smothering him, a bear that grew heavier as the hot days of midsummer settled upon the mesa.

This morning seemed no different from any other, at least in the beginning. The boy lay wrapped in his corded rabbit-fur blanket and watched through the open doorway as the sun god stretched, rose from behind the still snow-capped eastern mountains and began his daily journey across the sky trail.

In the shadows of the mud-plastered room, Little Otter's baby sister, Shell Flower, cooed to herself in her cradleboard. His mother hummed as she put a few sticks of wood on the coals in the fire pit. He heard the voices of his father and the other men of the village as they sang the greeting to the morning and sprinkled sacred cornmeal outside the doorways of their homes in the four sprawling community houses grouped about an uneven square on top of the mesa. The great houses were built of porous, fawn-colored rock. With their rows of rooms side by side and several stories high, they looked like giant stairsteps to the sky.

So much noise, Little Otter thought. He covered his head with his blanket and grunted irritably.

Later Blue Corn, slender and graceful, fed the baby while Little Otter and Pine Tip, his father, sat cross-

legged on the hard clay floor to eat. Using flat corn
cakes as scoops, they dipped into the pot of cold cooked
hominy. When he had finished, Pine Tip sucked his
fingers clean. Although he was sturdy, he was not tall.
Still, he had to bend to look out the low doorway.

"The rains, when will they begin? Such a task it is to
fill jars and carry water to the corn. But soon we must
do it if the rains do not come."

Suddenly, while rolling up the blankets, Blue Corn
gave a surprised squeal. Her braids swung wide as she
grabbed her broom of bound grasses and flailed at a
black, leggy creature on the floor.

"Stop! Enough!" Pine Tip coughed in the dust his
wife had raised. He squatted, picked up the spider between two fingers and threw it outside. "It has been
dead, I think, for some time. It falls apart." There was
a glint of amusement in his dark eyes; a deepening of
the wrinkles rayed out from their corners; a barely
contained quirk to his straight, firm lips.

"Don't laugh. It frightened me. It was dead? How
then did it get into the blanket?"

Both turned at the same moment and looked at
Little Otter. He was grinning, his hand held over his
mouth to smother his giggles. Blue Corn swung the
broom again.

"Oh! Ai!" screeched Little Otter, ducking his head
against the blows. "It was a joke!"

"If you play such a joke again, you'll sleep outside
with the dogs!" Blue Corn began to sweep the floor
vigorously. Over the swish of the broom, she asked
Pine Tip, "Have the people not done all things correctly? The dances? The prayers? It *must* rain. What
have we done wrong? Surely the gods will not send us
three bad years in a row."

"Who can know the minds of the gods? Perhaps we

have omitted something important without knowing
it." Pine Tip rubbed his hand across his square, red-
brown jaw, his high-bridged nose. His eyes searched
the sky for clouds. "The animals, those of the mountains and forest, already come close. The dryness brings
them. Yesterday I saw a mountain sheep standing on a
cliff. It looked at me. It was long ago, when Little Otter
was small, that I last saw one."

Little Otter dipped his hand into the pot again.
With his mouth full, he said, "It is big and strong.
Very great horns. Many times have I seen it."

"Truly? How long ago the first time?"

"Uhh, it was early spring." The boy jumped up, his
face suddenly set and still. "I go to the fields." He
ducked through the doorway and was gone.

"What is wrong with him?" Blus Corn asked. "Either
he's angry and doesn't speak, or he plays silly jokes, or
he runs away by himself."

"It is Leaping Deer. Still the boy mourns him."
Pine Tip struck his fist against the wall. "I too. He was
a good man. A trusted friend. Sometimes I think he
isn't gone. I feel him near."

"Don't talk like that! It's not right. You will hold
him from the gods. If you keep him in your thoughts,
how can he join the ancient ones? For his sake, for
Leaping Deer, let him go!"

Little Otter ran down the path away from the village. His mouth was twisted. Tears streamed down his
cheeks. Swerving, he climbed over rocks into one of the
small caves that pitted the canyon wall rising beside the
trail. In its dark recess he curled into a ball, hugging
his knees and rocking back and forth. Once again the
familiar wave of loneliness, the gnawing pain of re-
membering overwhelmed him.

Leaping Deer! Tall, handsome, kind. No one could best him in wrestling, in shooting the arrow, in planting corn. Never would Little Otter forget the awful sound of the deep, tearing coughs that had shaken his godfather's body or the heat from his flushed skin on that day when he had stumbled down from the high mesas, calling for help. Nor could he forget the strength of Leaping Deer's grasp on his shoulder, or the look of gratitude and affection in his fevered eyes. Slowly, carefully, they had descended the steep path, the man leaning heavily on the boy. Later, Leaping Deer had talked wildly, saying things that made no sense. He had coughed blood. And on the third day he had died, in spite of all the chants, the prayers, the ministrations of the curing society.

Even though summer had come, Little Otter's grief was still fresh. Every task renewed it, for he had learned each one with Leaping Deer. All things reminded him of his loss. This morning it was the mention of the mountain sheep, for he had first seen it on the very day his godfather had died. As he wandered across the mesas in stunned sorrow, his eyes had been drawn upward. There on a pinnacle of rock had stood the sheep, alone, majestic, watching him. Since then he had seen it often, always from a distance. Somehow, its presence comforted him.

Now the sound of voices, the rattle of rocks on the trail outside recalled him to the present. He looked out. The men and boys were coming down to work in the fields in the canyon. Little Otter snorted in disgust as he saw one of the boys push another toward the edge of the cliff, then pull him back just before he fell over. It was the sort of thing Gray Squirrel did all the time. What a bully he was! And how many times had Little Otter himself been the butt of his small cruelties!

Savagely, he thought, Someday I'll get even with Gray Squirrel. I don't care if he is bigger. Just because he's thirteen and will soon be initiated into his father's society, he is no better than we are. I'll show him. He'll see he can't push us around all the time.

He waited until the group passed. Then he rubbed the tears from his cheeks, and he too walked down to the fields.

ANGRY WORDS

The sun's midafternoon glare was hot on Little Otter's back as he bent over the tender young corn and squash plants. He picked caterpillars off leaves and pulled weeds. Heat reflected from the cliffs on each side. The breezes did not cool the air here as they did in the village above. Down across the fields, other boys and men weeded industriously. Like him, they wore only breech-clouts, and their brown skin glistened in the sun. He heard them call jokingly to one another.

How can they be so happy? he thought. They were Leaping Deer's friends. Have they forgotten so soon?

Frowning, he stood up and arched his back to ease the strain. To the east, through a cleft between two mesas, he saw the jagged mountains beyond the valley of the great river. Behind him, to the west, the rounded green peaks of the lower mountain range pushed their heads above the plateau, which was a flat tableland split into many deep canyons and broken mesas. He wished he were high in those mountains. Up there in the summer, the forests were like cool, green caves. Swift streams bubbled clear and cold, falling down high cliffs into the canyons. He licked his dry lips. Just thinking of the frothing waterfalls made him thirsty.

A sudden movement at his feet caught his attention. He bent and with a quick swoop captured a slender striped lizard with a long tail. The tiny feet scrabbled at his palm. Gently the boy turned the lizard over. With one grubby finger he stroked its soft white belly and pulsing throat. It lay charmed, motionless.

Little Otter grinned a funny, turned-down smile. Carrying his captive, he crossed the field. At the foot of a piñon pine he found the large water jar that was always left there for those who worked among the crops. Hidden by the tree, Little Otter lifted the lid, drank deeply and set the jar down. Then he slipped the lizard inside it and replaced the lid. He jumped as a blue jay alighted on a nearby branch and cawed loudly.

"Hush! Don't tell!" He waved his arms, and the bird flew away, still cawing.

Struck by another idea, Little Otter glanced quickly around, then knelt on the sandy ground in front of a large rock. He dug busily for a minute, put something in the hole and carefully smoothed the ground again. He stood and looked critically at the place, then nodded in satisfaction. Chuckling to himself, he returned to the field.

A few minutes later he heard Deep Lake, the War Chief of the village, call, "Does anyone want a drink? Let's rest a bit." The workers gathered in the shade of the trees. Little Otter carefully timed his arrival to be among the last.

Deep Lake removed the lid, lifted the jar and drank. Then he held it for Snow Feather, next to him. Again it was tilted. Suddenly Snow Feather made a strangled sound and tumbled backward. Water splashed across his chest. A long, thin tail hung from Snow Feather's mouth. He sputtered, pulled out the lizard and tossed it away. Then he rubbed furiously at his mouth with the back of his hand.

"Yah! Awful!"

The lizard skittered away into a pile of rocks. Little Otter peered down into the jar. His voice was innocent.

"Humm . . . Funny. How did he get there? Are there any others?"

Casually, he took a drink and passed the jug on. The others, with suspicious glances, took careful sips. When Gray Squirrel's turn came, he cupped his hand and threw some of the water at Little Otter.

"Here, puppy! To make you grow."

Little Otter squared off angrily, but already Gray Squirrel had turned away. "You should have seen how you looked," he taunted Snow Feather. "Water all over you! And that tail sticking out of your mouth, it looked so funny!" He slapped Snow Feather on the back so hard he knocked the smaller boy to his knees. Then he hooted with laughter.

"Let him alone! How is it that you only pick on boys smaller than you?" Little Otter stood with clenched fists planted on his hips.

Gray Squirrel was so surprised he stared with his mouth wide open. Little Otter deliberately walked over to the big rock and slid down as though to sit at its base. This infuriated the older boy, who jumped forward and roughly shoved Little Otter aside.

"You can't sit there! Son of a foreigner, you know that's my place!"

Gray Squirrel dropped heavily to the ground.

"Aiee!" he screamed instantly, and rolled over, making frantic motions. A small, round cactus stuck to his bare backside, held firmly by sharp, hooked spines driven deep into the flesh.

"Get it off! Get it off!"

Deep Lake held him down while one of the other men pulled the cactus free. One by one, the needles were removed. Little Otter and Snow Feather, joined by the other boys, gasped and shouted with laughter. Even the men smiled or chuckled. Gray Squirrel was not the most popular youth in the village.

When he was finally released, the injured boy confronted Little Otter. "You did it! You hid that cactus under the sand. You know I always sit there."

"Lucky for me you pushed me away. *I* might have sat on it. I don't like cactus needles, especially in *me*."

Gray Squirrel advanced. "I'll break your head open!"

Deep Lake stepped between them. "No fighting! Those who quarrel among themselves have no strength left for their enemies. The gods will punish if necessary. Gray Squirrel, do not seek trouble. You make a big thing out of a little bad luck."

Pushing his face a few inches from Little Otter's nose, Gray Squirrel muttered, "Bad luck! Maybe *he* calls it that, but *I* don't. Your mother, *she* makes our bad luck. Foreigners, both of you. Go away, or you'll be sorry."

Little Otter sucked in his breath at the ugly tone of the threat. His lips tightened to a thin line. He fairly spat out his words. "That cactus—I wish it had been a rattlesnake!"

The two boys glared at each other. They had just made a declaration of war, and they both knew it. Then Little Otter stalked away, stiff-backed. He would work no more in the fields that day.

His anger swelling like a bubble within him, he ran

up a small hill, jumped a couple of tiny streams and clambered over a pile of rocks. Scrambling up hand-and-footholds carved in the soft rock of the cliff, he climbed to a wide ledge extending along the whole south face of the mesa. The ledge formed a broad pathway dividing the cave dwellings in the canyon from the village at the top. Many trails, some worn knee-deep in the stone, branched off from the ledge in different directions.

Little Otter looked back down the main path to the small pool at the bottom where the women filled their water jars. Squash Blossom, his father's aunt, was just beginning the climb. She was old and bony, her shoulders drooped; but she could still balance a tall jug on her head. She toiled up the steep slope.

Above the spot where Little Otter stood, the path curved and passed between two huge boulders. On impulse, he slipped behind one of the great rocks. In a few minutes he heard the slow scrape, scrape of Squash Blossom's sandals. She rounded the curve and entered the shadow of the boulders. Suddenly Little Otter jumped out in front of her.

"Hoo!"

"Ai!" She stepped backward and threw up her arms. The jar on her head teetered and fell. It struck the boulder, breaking into many pieces.

"Little Otter! How you frightened me!"

Little Otter stared at the wreckage. The pot had been beautiful—white with black wavy designs painted on the fat sides and around the handles. The bubble of anger within him burst. It drained away like the water running down the path.

"I'm sorry! Truly. I only meant to . . ." He hung his head.

"Now I must get another jar and fill it. My mother

used to say that to have to do a thing over is more a burden to the heart than to the hands." Squash Blossom's voice was sweet and soft. Her thin brown face, covered with a network of wrinkles, shone with perspiration. Her black bangs clung damply to her forehead. She leaned against the rock.

Little Otter touched her arm. "Please sit here. It is shady. I'm so sorry. I'll get another jar and fill it for you."

"What if someone laughs to see you do woman's work?"

"Let them! I care not."

He ran up the path, mumbling to himself. What got into me? he thought. I'm getting to be as bad as Gray Squirrel. Squash Blossom is kind and good. She is the only woman in the village who is a true friend to my mother.

From the time he had been a small boy, he could remember Squash Blossom always being there when she was needed. She was a widow. Having no children, she lived alone in one small room. Pine Tip, her nephew, saw that she did not go hungry. Little Otter had always been a favorite of hers. He could count on her for a small treat of honey cake or roasted pine nuts whenever he presented himself at her door.

I'll make it up to her for the broken pot, he thought. I'll go hunting. I'll bring back a rabbit for her stewpot.

Little Otter rounded a corner and entered the square of community houses. A few scrawny, short-legged dogs basked in the sun. Noisy, naked babies, tended by older sisters, climbed over doorsills and played in the thick dust. Their mothers watched their children and worked at the same time, sitting on the ground before their homes or upon the flat roofs. They gossiped while they made clay pots or twisted fibers into cording or plaited sandals from yucca leaves. The hurrying boy gave them only a passing glance. He knew his mother was not among them. She never was.

He reached Squash Blossom's room and found a jar, and then he went across to his own home. There he collected his bow and arrows and throwing stick. Shell Flower, his baby sister, was asleep in her cradleboard, which was hanging from the rafters, but his mother was not there.

Little Otter filled the jar at the spring and then carried it up to Squash Blossom. She was still resting beneath a piñon tree. Beside her was Blue Corn, a net bag filled with wild greens from the stream beds in her lap.

With an embarrassed, sidewise glance at his mother, Little Otter handed the dripping jar to Squash Blossom. "I told her I was sorry, Mother. Now I go to hunt. I finished most of the weeding."

Blue Corn nodded. "Meat would taste good. Be careful! Why not take another with you? If one got hurt, the other could go for help. Snow Feather, perhaps. He misses your company, I know."

"It's better by myself." Little Otter crossed the ledge and disappeared down the hand-and-foothold ladder.

Blue Corn gave an exasperated sigh. "What can we do? He is unhappy, yes. But he has changed. He rebels so. And his pranks! Each time I shake out the bedcoverings, a frog, a beetle, a spider jumps at me. This morning, with the spider, oh, how angry I was! And now your jar. It's a shame."

"I can make other jars. He is, after all, only a boy. It is hard even for us older ones to trust the wisdom of the gods."

"True. Sometimes I feel that if he would talk to

someone about it . . . Pine Tip tries, but Little Otter runs away by himself. It is as though my son were lost. Lost *inside*, I mean."

"My mother used to say that time and love, not anger, heal grief. But how hard it is to learn that lesson!"

Squash Blossom's repetitions of her mother's sayings would have been tiresome had they not been said with such sweet, grave sincerity.

Then she added with a hard edge of bitterness that surprised Blue Corn, "But the fault, it is not all with him. How badly the people have treated him, and you! Fifteen years, Blue Corn! Fifteen years since Pine Tip brought you here. One would think after all this time . . ."

Blue Corn knew that only great depths of feeling could have caused such an outburst. The village women usually kept their anger, if any, held tightly within themselves. She laid her small hand on the cracked, work-hardened hand of the older woman.

"Say no more. As you have told me so often, we must leave it to the gods." She smiled. "Remember when I came? I think I was as lost then as Little Otter is now. If you had not been here, if you had not welcomed me . . . But even you did not know how often I thought of going back, of crossing the mountains again to rejoin my own people."

"But you stayed."

"Yes." Blue Corn's smile turned down at the corners like her son's. "Does one ever give up hope?" She lifted her bag of greens. "Are you ready? Shell Flower will be awake. She is a hungry little one."

"This old person will rest a while longer."

Blue Corn nodded. "Tomorrow I go for clay to make pots. I will bring enough for you also."

She smoothed her long, straight cotton dress, draped

to leave one slim shoulder and both arms bare. She was more slightly built than the heavyset, square-faced women of this village, but she had a look of strength and pride in the lift of her head and in the carriage of her shoulders. As she walked up the path, her small, sandaled feet touched the ground lightly. Squash Blossom looked after her, shaking her head.

How beautiful she is! Squash Blossom thought. I wish I could help more. But what can one do?

A DISAPPEARANCE
AND A DISCOVERY

It was late afternoon when Little Otter started home from his hunting. He carried two small rabbits and a prairie dog—all he had to show for three hours of crossing and recrossing the mesas and flats. Reaching the next mesa to the one on which the village stood, he climbed out to the very end and perched there among the rocks.

This was one of his favorite retreats. The cliffs here dropped in almost sheer walls to the talus slopes and canyons far below. From his perch he could see the shadow that marked the far edge of the plateau. Beyond the mesas lay a great valley, and beyond it the eastern mountains. The valley stretched north and south farther than a man could see. Through the middle of it wound the shining, sunstruck curves of the big river.

The plateau had been the home of his people for uncounted generations. Hidden in its canyons and sleeping on its mesas were many brush-covered mounds of rock or smoke-blackened caves, remnants of family dwellings or small communities now abandoned and almost forgotten.

When I am grown, Little Otter thought, I'll go a long way from here. There are so many places to see. Maybe I'll even go to my mother's village on the other side of the western mountains. Why should I stay here? Leaping Deer is gone. I don't belong. Father has traveled. Mother too. Why not I?

The rattle of a dislodged stone interrupted his dreaming. He looked around just in time to see a boy dodge behind a clump of bushes an arrow's shot away.

"Gray Squirrel!" he exclaimed softly—and thought, I can't let him trap me out here. A push or a stumble and one of us will end up on the rocks at the bottom of the cliff.

He considered quickly. Extending from a spot close to the other boy's hiding place and ending near Little Otter's perch was a long gash that cut through the bedrock. Surely Gray Squirrel, planning a surprise, would creep along the bottom of that natural ditch. It was the only way to get close without being seen.

To reach the trail down the cliff to the village, Little Otter had to cross that ditch. Gray Squirrel would be after him in a flash. Even if he made it to the path, his pursuer could roll stones on him from above. No, that way was too dangerous.

Let's see, Little Otter thought. During the time he's in the ditch, I won't be able to see him. But—and now he grinned—Gray Squirrel won't be able to see what I do, either.

Once—until it had been destroyed, years before, by a landslide—there had been a trail down into the canyon on the other side of the mesa. It had led to a small cave, halfway down the cliff, where ceremonies had been held by their ancestors. One day Little Otter and Leaping Deer had become curious about the old cave. In their search for a way to reach it, they had discovered a tiny, precipitous track now hidden by a tangle of scrub oak. If he could get to it . . .

Pretending he had not seen the other boy, Little Otter stretched lazily, yawned and lay down on the rock, his head cradled on his bent arm. By peeping between his arm and the rock, he could see the far end of the ditch. With his other hand he grasped his bow and arrows and throwing stick. He waited.

There was a flicker of movement behind the bushes. His hand tightened. Suddenly Gray Squirrel left cover and dashed to the ditch. Little Otter grinned. He had guessed correctly. Now! He silently bounded across to the pine tree that marked the top of the small trail. Pushing the branches aside, he slid over the edge. With both hands full of weapons and game kill, he could not steady himself. For a dizzying moment he hung in space. Then, desperate, he twisted. His feet found the path. In a few more moments he was safe inside the cave. He leaned back against the wall and caught his breath.

Opposite him he saw paintings on the rock: hunters stalking a deer. Farther down the wall there was another. It was of a dancer with feathers sticking up from the mask that covered his head. Laughing to himself, Little Otter did a little stamping dance step. Oh, to see Gray Squirrel's face! he thought. How puzzled he'll be! He'll think I floated right up into the air!

Shadows were slowly filling the valley when Little Otter left the cave. His glee had evaporated. He was cross again. It had all been so much trouble. Besides, he was hungry. He crawled carefully over boulders, inching his way along the side of the cliff until he rounded the end of the mesa. On the other side he found a slope that was not too steep to descend. He watched for a while. No one moved on the floor of the canyon. Gray Squirrel had surely gone home by this time. Digging in his heels, Little Otter slid down a bank of deep sand and gravel.

Later he would think back to this time, What if I had chosen another place to go down? What if I hadn't paid attention? For when he reached the bottom of the slope, he heard an odd sound, the soft whimpering of an animal.

It is a dog, he thought, listening. It sounds hurt.

He stood motionless, his eyes exploring the talus on either side. Again he heard the whimper. Quietly, he crept closer. Suddenly he saw the twitch of a large, pointed ear. He dropped his game and weapons. In another moment he was bending over, looking into a crevice between two rocks.

"Why, it's a coyote! A young one."

The coyote stared at him with yellow eyes. It lifted its lip in a snarl, baring its sharp white teeth.

Little Otter laughed. "You sound so fierce. Are you stuck? Hold still. I will lift you out. Ai! Don't snap! Why, I know you! You're the one with the piece out of your ear."

Squatting beside the frightened pup's head, Little Otter soothed it with low crooning. "You are a pretty one. Your coat is as golden as the newly risen moon on a summer night. There now, I won't hurt you."

Soon the animal allowed Little Otter to stroke it. After a longer time he slowly slipped first one hand and then the other under the soft, furry body. Gently he lifted it. The coyote yelped, but she didn't bite.

"I think maybe you remember me. Poor little one! Your leg, it's broken. No wonder you couldn't free yourself."

The pup was now half grown. When Little Otter stood, her thick, bushy tail with its crisp black tip hung

down almost to his knees. She was a heavy armful. He skirted a field of beans and headed toward a long split in the cliff ahead. The split hid narrow steps and gouged-out hand-and-toeholds leading to the village above. Panting from his effort and sticky with sweat, he laid the pup in the cool dust beneath the low branches of a pine at the base of the cliff. Then back he went to retrieve his weapons and the results of his hunting.

When he returned, he laid the prairie dog in front of the pup's nose. She sniffed it, then tore at it hungrily.

"You'll be safe here. I'll bring water. And Father too, if he'll come. He will know how to fix your leg. Don't crawl away. Now, listen, please! Stay here!"

The boy climbed quickly to the top of the mesa. "Is Father here?" he asked, stepping over the raised door-step of his home. His eyes, accustomed to the sunlight, saw only shadows in the windowless room.

Blue Corn, who had just finished brushing and plait-ing her hair, tossed her long braids back over her shoulders. "No, my son. Look at the end of the mesa toward the sunrise."

Little Otter hung his weapons on rafter pegs and gave the two rabbits to his mother. "One for us and one, if you agree, for Squash Blossom, to make up for breaking her water jar. I go to find Father."

He hurried out, and his mother crossed to the door-way. What had happened? He sounded different, ex-cited. Only this morning she had laid a cornmeal trail and sung a prayer that her son become happy again. Had the gods answered her so soon? She smiled as she picked up the rabbit to take to Pine Tip's aunt.

Little Otter went through the village and around and between several circular, flat-topped kivas. These were roofed pits sunk halfway into the ground. They were combined workshops, worship centers and clubhouses for the men. An outside ladder led from the ground up to the roof of each kiva, where another ladder with very long side poles extended through a center hole to the large, dark high-ceilinged chamber below.

In the kivas the men gathered to prepare for dances, to repair the masks of the gods, to perform special rites, to initiate new members into the village societies or just to visit and tell stories. In a year or two, Little Otter thought, I will take my place among them. Then I can do as I please. And Gray Squirrel will have nothing left to boast about.

Leaving the town behind, he ran past the pens of the sacred turkeys and the cage where the old bald eagle was tied to his perch. The eagle, the "chieftain-bird," was the best and strongest representative of the powerful sky god. Little Otter shivered as he saw the old bird's head turn to watch him. He felt as though the dark, glittering eyes were shooting tiny arrows into his back. The turkeys were sometimes eaten, but the eagles, never. The feathers of all were used in ceremonials. Little Otter wished sometimes that the old eagle were not so sacred. If there was one bird he would enjoy eating in a stew, it was that one.

He found his father sitting with a group of other men. They were skillfully shaping stone arrowheads or scrapers, axes or knives. A few quick blows of stone on stone, then gentle pressure from a pointed deer antler, and a beautiful arrowhead lay in a strong brown hand. For stone they used obsidian, the black, flaking glass from the mountains; or basalt from the mesas; or quartz from the riverbeds. Flint was rare and highly prized. Sometimes, if they were lucky, they were able to trade for it with the tribes who hunted the buffalo on the plains beyond the eastern mountains.

When Pine Tip turned to him, Little Otter said, "Father, your son has need of you. I have something to show you. A knife is needed too."

Pine Tip, with a surprised look, nodded to the men, then rose and followed. Minutes later, he squatted and peered through the piñon branches.

"So! For this you bring me here. A coyote! And of such a different color. You know what a nuisance they are."

Little Otter placed a gourd of water under the pup's nose. She lapped thirstily.

"But Father, the leg. To leave her here would be to feed her to a wolf or mountain lion."

"Small loss!"

"She's so pretty, isn't she? And already she becomes tame. See, she licks my hand. Please, Father?"

"But a coyote! We cannot allow them in the village. You know that."

"Not in the village, Father. And only until her leg heals."

Pine Tip looked at Little Otter's pleading face. "I should not do it. You understand that if she stays close, she will cause mischief. It is unthinkable that our corn should be stolen from the fields, especially this year when every grain is precious. If I do fix the leg . . . When she runs again, you must set her free. Once she is well, she must go."

"Yes, Father." Little Otter grinned. "Now I'll hold her muzzle closed so you can fix the leg."

When the leg had been splinted with pine bark held on by thin bark strips, Pine Tip stood up. "There! By the time of the new moon she will be as strong as ever. Where will you keep her?"

"One of those deep holes near the black canyon should do. With heavy boughs across the top, she cannot climb out and nothing can get in to hurt her."

"And food?"

"I gave her a prairie dog. Tomorrow I'll hunt again. There are lots of toads and lizards around."

"Lizards," Pine Tip said thoughtfully. "Ah, yes. You seem to have no difficulty finding such small creatures. Deep Lake told me there was one today in the water jar at the cornfield."

Little Otter stared at his toes.

"My son, my son"—and Pine Tip cleared his throat. "I know you miss Leaping Deer. So do I. But to act like a child—is that what he taught you?"

The boy shook his head. Had his father also heard about the cactus? Pine Tip's next words removed any doubt.

"And another thing—to play a prank that hurts. That is not like you. It leads to other things. We can't have trouble between you boys."

"But Gray Squirrel thinks he's better than anyone else."

"To prove him false you must act better, not worse, than he. True?"

Little Otter nodded slowly, shifting from one foot to the other. Then he said abruptly, "Father, how did you get that scar on your leg? I think you told me once, but I've forgotten."

Pine Tip blinked. A smile began in his eyes as he allowed the conversation to veer in a different direction. His son was a master at changing the subject.

"As I said before, one thing leads to another. We cannot see the ending in the beginning. I got this on a bear hunt with your mother's brothers. It was long ago."

"The bear clawed you?"

A chuckle. "No, this clumsy one stumbled and rolled

down a steep bank in the darkness. A splintery tree
stub slashed me as I fell." He rubbed the long white
scar below his knee. "Many moons my leg took to heal
—so long that I had to spend the whole winter in the
village on the other side of the mountains."

"Mother's home village?"

"Yes. Your mother's father was the chief then. He
insisted I stay in his home. Your mother and I learned
to care for each other. The next spring your mother
came here with me."

"Why did she leave? There she was a person of importance, a member of the Antelope clan. Here, you
know how they treat her." Little Otter bent to a heap
of broken pots at the bottom of the cliff and picked up
a fragment. "This is Mother's. One can always tell her
bowls. She cannot even use the same designs as the
others. It's cruel."

"True. But minds are changed from inside, not outside. One cannot force people to think differently." He
sighed. "How young we were! It did not occur to us
to question how others would feel. And once on our
way, we would not turn back. We were stubborn too."

He sat silent for a short while. Then he stood up,
saying in a determinedly cheerful tone, "Your mother
will wonder why we are not there for our meal."

"I'll find a safe place for the coyote. Then I'll come."

Pine Tip nodded and walked toward the cliff steps.

Pine Tip's back was brown and hard-muscled. His
long hair, brushed well by Blue Corn every evening,
was looped into a shining black knot at the back of his
head. When he walks, Little Otter thought, every step
is sure and steady. I can't imagine him not knowing
what to do. His walk is dignified, like the great river.
My mother's steps are quick, like a dancing mountain
stream.

Suddenly, on the edge of the far mesa, he saw a familiar silhouette. "Look, Father! The sheep!"

Pine Tip turned. "A fine sight!"

"Thank you for fixing the coyote's leg."

Pine Tip waved and started up the trail. He thought, It is I who should thank you. I'm glad you needed me, my son.

Again the boy lifted the coyote. He carried her through the wooded part of the little valley; across a stream bed, now dry in the summer heat, and into a narrow canyon at the head of a deeper one walled with sharp black rock. He found the natural pits as he remembered them. Laying the coyote beside one, he jumped down into it. Then he carefully lifted the pup and laid her in the bottom.

"There! When I pull branches over the top, you'll be safe. Don't worry. I'll take care of you."

He knelt beside her. She nuzzled his hand. He stroked her unusual yellow fur. "So beautiful! Your coat and your eyes are as golden as the willow leaves in the fall and the slender new branches in the spring. I'll call you Willow."

The coyote made a contented whining sound. The black tip of her thick, fluffy tail began to flick back and forth. Suddenly Little Otter laughed.

"Gray Squirrel! He would be so angry if he knew. If it had not been for him, I would never have found you. I'll have to be very careful. If he found out about you, he would spoil everything."

ThE WORLD
OF WILLOW

The days of high summer went swiftly. Each morning Little Otter completed his chores as quickly as possible. Then he hunted for food for Willow. Blue Corn had a respite from the crawling or jumping creatures in the bedcoverings; those now reached Willow's hungry stomach instead. Little Otter was too occupied with his new pet to play as many pranks as usual, and the whole village breathed easier.

Twice Willow chewed off the bark strips on her leg, and Little Otter had to retie them. Nevertheless, the leg seemed to be healing well and straight. Soon she could put her weight upon it, and one day Little Otter found her standing on her hind feet, stretching with her front legs toward the top of the hole.

"You're growing as fast as the weeds in the fields," he said as he dropped down beside her and scratched her head behind her ears. "Be careful! The leg might break again."

"Hello, Little Otter. So this is your coyote."

"Oh, Mother! You startled me."

"I've been gathering cactus fruit. I wanted to see your pet before you freed her."

Blue Corn dropped her bag of dark red fruit and leaned the cradleboard, containing a bright-eyed Shell Flower, against a rock. She sat down beside the hole.

"How intelligent she looks!"

"She is very smart, this one."

"My brother had a pet coyote for a while."

"What happened to it?"

"A mountain lion, perhaps. Who knows? But that one was the color of dust, like most—not golden like yours."

Little Otter climbed out of the hole and sat with her. "You have four brothers, haven't you?"

"Yes. They are all older than I. Cloud had the coyote. Standing Bear may be chief of our village now. I wish I could hear news of them."

"My father, where did he meet them?"

"At the eastern salt lakes where men from many villages gather salt. One of the group spoke both languages. Friendships were made. Pine Tip returned with my brothers to visit our country. Only for a short time, you understand. Then he was to return to the plateau here by crossing the mountains instead of by the usual trail along the great river."

"But he was hurt. He stayed the winter."

"Yes."

"Your mother and father—when you left with him, what did they say?"

Blue Corn gazed at the distant blue mountains. "I don't know. We ran away. I have heard nothing since."

"Did it frighten you to come here among strangers?"

"To this foolish one it was an adventure. Like a tale told by the old ones. A chance to outwit fierce Navajos and Apaches, to fight off wild forest animals." She smiled, looking very young. "It was really a very quiet trip, until we got here."

"What then?"

Blue Corn shook her head. "I suppose I had been spoiled by my parents, my brothers. I was used to something else, something quite different."

Little Otter let dust slip through his fingers. Then he stared at the village on the mesa. "I hate them all! Never to let you be a member of a society! Or to use their pottery designs! Or to dance in the dances!"

"You must not talk so. Never hate, my son. Hate is a sickness. It eats the heart. The ways of the gods are strange. Often a man cannot understand them."

They sat in silence for a few moments. Then Little Otter said, "Mother . . . ?"

"Yes?"

"If the choice were yours again, what then?"

Blue Corn thought. Then she answered, "What is done is done. That is all that matters. Each day must be lived so that it becomes a good memory. What better way to live is there?"

She stood up, swinging the cradleboard to her back. "I've stayed too long. Your coyote, she is very pretty. But do not let your heart become entangled. She must soon go free."

"I know, Mother."

But already Little Otter found it hard to imagine what life would be like without the golden coyote.

Before many days passed, he found out. One afternoon when Little Otter arrived with an offering of mice and ground squirrels, the hole was empty! Willow was gone! Never had the boy known such loneliness as flooded over him then. First Leaping Deer had left him. Now Willow also. He felt as deserted as if he were the only person left on the plateau—even in the whole world.

He shook his fists in the air. "It was a bear or moun-

tain lion! That is what happened. She is dead! I'm sure
she is. Oh, Willow!"

He stamped around, picking up stones and smashing
them down again. Finally, however, he became calm
enough to think more reasonably. He began to look for
signs of what had really occurred.

"There is no blood, no fur, no sign of struggle." It
could not have been another animal after all. For a
moment he felt a great relief. But as he looked further,
this was followed by heartsickness.

The branches on top of the pit looked as if they had
been thrust aside. He got down on his knees and examined the hole more closely. Now he saw the long claw
marks in the soft rock of the side walls. The coyote had
worked and struggled for a long while to get out. She
had left of her own free will. Could Willow really have
wanted to go? There was nothing else he could think.

Little Otter sat down in the dust. Tears welled up.
Fiercely, he brushed them away. Willow had left him.

He said defiantly, "Why should I care about that one?
She didn't care about me. If she had, she wouldn't have
gone away. I should have known. She was too old when I
found her, too old to be really tamed."

Still the tears brimmed over. He had not known until
then how much he loved her. For a long time he lay on
the ground, one arm thrown over his face. The afternoon shadows deepened and grew cool.

Suddenly something cold and wet thrust against his
ribs. "Oh!" Little Otter's heart thumped, and he jerked
his arm from his eyes. Willow was looking down into his
face, her tongue lolling out.

The boy's eyes widened until they looked like shiny
black moons. Giving a joyous shout, he threw his arms
around Willow's neck. The sunlight gleamed on her
beautiful golden back and on the thick, plumed tail that

waved back and forth like a pine branch whipping in
the wind.

"You didn't go after all," he whispered into the
pointed ear with the little notch out of it. "You were
free, but you didn't go. I think you love me too." He
laughed as she licked the tears from his face.

Then began the happy afternoons: the hours of
roving and romping about the mesas, of hunting and
playing, or of napping in the shade of a piñon pine with
the cloud shadows moving slowly across the plateau and
the air heavy with the scent of warm juniper.

Mornings in the fields sped by for the boy. He
worked fast, though not as thoroughly as he should
have. He hurried to be with Willow, and he told himself no one would notice if he missed a few weeds or
neglected to water a row of melons.

Once with the coyote, he forgot everything else; even
Gray Squirrel's frequent teasing—for the older boy
never missed an opportunity to poke, trip or taunt
Little Otter. Away from the village, Little Otter and
Willow lived in a separate world of their own. It was a
world of sun and warmth, of comradeship and excitement and love.

There was the day, for instance, when they saw a
great eagle soaring above them. "Hide!" Little Otter
called, running to crouch in a nearby cave. "If the great
one is hungry enough, he might come for you. Hide,
Willow!"

The truth was that he himself was frightened. He
knelt with his arm around the coyote's neck, and they
watched from the shelter of the cave as the huge bird
circled lower and lower, finally alighting upon a dead
pine near the edge of a canyon. It held a cottontail
rabbit in the long, curved talons of one foot. When the

eagle dropped from sight over the canyon rim, Little
Otter and Willow went elsewhere to hunt.

For her den Willow chose a small, secluded cave near
the village. If she was within hearing, she usually came
when Little Otter blew on a thin bone whistle. Sometimes, though, she lurked playfully in the bushes until
the boy began to walk away. Then she silently crept up
behind him, launched herself at the back of his knees
and tumbled him to the ground. What a mock battle
they would have! Such a din of barking and snarling,
shouting and laughing! Breathless and hot, they would
roll over and over until they were covered with dust.

Little Otter was so happy now that he was surprised
sometimes to realize he hadn't thought of Leaping Deer
for several days. It was getting harder and harder for
him to remember exactly what his godfather had looked
like. Still, he didn't feel guilty. Leaping Deer, he was
sure, would have understood better than anyone else
how he felt about Willow.

Their hunting expeditions were successful, for Willow had uncanny speed and quick, sharp teeth, and
Little Otter was skillful with his bow and arrows and
throwing stick. When he was training the coyote, the
boy discovered one thing: he could never come up
behind her and touch her unexpectedly. She would
whirl and snap; and the boy knew her wild instincts
were still strong.

He taught her to bring him the rabbits she caught
beyond her own need. This led to one of her favorite
tricks. She delighted in dropping a rabbit just beyond
his reach. When he stooped to pick it up, she grabbed
it again and placed it a little farther away. Over and
over she would do it. Finally, when she sensed that he
was tired of playing, she would carry it casually over

and drop it on top of his foot. Then she would go back to her hunting.

Blue Corn was glad to have the wild game. "You have much luck these days," she said. Little Otter only nodded, careful not to tell her his pet made most of the kills.

Once Pine Tip asked, "The coyote, is she well again?"

"Yes, Father. You fixed her leg perfectly."

"Did you turn her loose?"

"She is free."

"Good. I have worried about her. She was too close to the cornfields."

Little Otter quieted his conscience with the knowledge that he had told the truth, even if not the whole truth. Willow *was* free. If she chose to stay near him, it was not his fault, was it? He asked himself what Leaping Deer would have said, but his mind skittered away from the answer.

Then one evening when he was coming home through a canyon south of the village, his quarrel with Gray Squirrel flared up again. Rounding a bend, he found the older boy blocking his path.

"This time you'll not disappear!"

"How do you know?" Little Otter asked. "Maybe I can fly through the air like a raven."

Gray Squirrel looked uneasy for a moment. Then he blustered, "I don't believe it. Here, give me those doves and quail! My luck was bad today. I don't understand how you find game. No one else can."

Little Otter backed away. Gray Squirrel rushed him, throwing him to the ground. They wrestled back and forth, first one on top, then the other. Suddenly Gray Squirrel jerked his elbow back hard, right into the pit of the younger boy's stomach. Little Otter doubled over, gasping for breath. Gray Squirrel grabbed the birds.

Standing over Little Otter, he jeered, "Why don't you fly away now?" He walked off with a swagger.

Little Otter was still sitting in the path, sputtering with anger, when Willow trotted around the bend and touched his arm questioningly with her long nose.

"Where have you been? Go get him! Go on, Willow! Get those birds!"

Willow looked from him to the other boy, now far down the path. She cocked her head. Finally she seemed to understand. She dashed after Gray Squirrel. She didn't make a sound as she crept up behind him and hurled herself at the back of his legs.

Gray Squirrel fell in a surprised heap. He rolled over and tried to sit up. Then he collapsed with a frightened howl. He threw his arms up to protect his face. A big yellow animal was standing over him snarling and whining. Little Otter ran up and squatted beside them. His grin was so wide it almost split his face. Willow growled and prodded Gray Squirrel's ribs with her paw. She couldn't understand why this new boy wouldn't play. All he did was scream.

"Little Otter, call it off! Help! Take your birds. Make it go away!"

"Will you let me alone after this? Will you stop bothering me?"

"Yes, yes! Anything! You must be a witch." His teeth began to chatter in fright. "B-b-but I won't t-t-tell. T-t-truly! Just g-g-get this creature off."

"All right. We'll let you go this time. Next time you won't be so lucky. If you make more trouble . . . If you tell anyone about this . . ."

Little Otter left the threat hanging in the air. He

bent and picked up the game. "Stay here awhile! Leaving too soon will bring the mountain lion who lives on that mesa. He's our friend too. He'll tear you apart if we say so."

When Little Otter looked back a few minutes later, Gray Squirrel was still sitting on the ground wiping his pale, perspiring face with shaking hands and looking up at the mesa.

Little Otter laughed. "He'll be there when the sun god wakes tomorrow. He's so scared that he doesn't see our real friend, the big mountain sheep, up there. If he did, he would know there is no mountain lion close by. Poor Gray Squirrel!"

A little farther on, he chuckled again. "Witches! How funny! One good thing: he won't follow us. And he won't find your den. If he really believes us to be witches, he'll stop pestering me, too. At least for a little while."

A SNAKE TRICK

The squashes on the vines were swelling into pale yellow globes, and the thin green ears of corn were filling out, when Pine Tip quietly broke the most exciting news of the summer. It was evening, and the family was in the one large room that was its combined living, cooking, dining and sleeping area. Blue Corn hovered over the small fire near the doorway. Little Otter and his father sat on the clay floor. They watched while Blue Corn ladled a thick meat mixture onto flat corn cakes, rolled them into succulent cylinders and put them into bowls. They ate in silence, until Pine Tip, satisfied at last, wiped his mouth with his hand.

"Good!"

Through the doorway he could see across the square to the end of the mesas, and across the valley of the great river to the high range on the other side. In the sunset the mountains glowed like a bank of pink cactus flowers.

"We had a meeting in the kiva today," he said. "We were so late in planting this spring that there are problems. The corn will not ripen at the usual time."

Blue Corn nodded. Little Otter helped himself to another corn cake.

"It was decided to go on a buffalo hunt. We need the meat badly. Instead of waiting until after harvest as we usually do, we will leave just after the next new moon."

"Why?"

"The harvest will be so delayed that if we went afterward, the winter might catch us on the plains. To leave soon is best. Then we should be back in time to bring in the corn from the fields. With help from the women, there will be enough boys and old men to care for the crops while we are gone."

He did not need to add, for it was something Blue Corn and Little Otter already knew well, that if there was an early frost, the corn would not ripen at all and many people would die of hunger before spring came again.

Little Otter jumped to his feet. "A buffalo hunt! Father, can I go? Please? Last year you said maybe I could. More than anything I want to go with you."

Pine Tip spoke reluctantly. "No, not this year either. You are still too young."

"Is Gray Squirrel going?"

His father nodded.

"But he is only a little older than I."

"True. It was not for me to decide. But remember, my son, age is not always measured by summers and winters. You are not yet ready. You don't think like a man."

"How does a man think?" Little Otter's face was stormy. "If you tell me, I can learn how to do it in time to go. I learn fast."

His father smiled, but his eyes were sober. "That I cannot teach you. Nobody can. Each must find for himself how to think like a man. When the time comes, you'll know. It is something that grows in the heart."

"But Father . . ."

"I'm sorry. Not this year." Pine Tip's tone was final.

Little Otter settled back in glum silence while Pine Tip discussed plans with Blue Corn.

"Seven days from today the men go into the kivas. For four days there we prepare for the buffalo dances. On the eleventh day from now, we have the dances. And the day after that, we leave. Our kinsmen from the village in the canyon to the west will go with us. If the hunting is good, we should bring dried meat, and warm buffalo-skin robes for the winter. And for next year's dances there will be new horned heads for the dancers to wear. All men who are able are going. Many strong backs will be needed to carry home the loads."

"You know those large nuts that grow on the plains?" Blue Corn asked. "The ones that are good to eat, that have husks that make fine brown dye? Can you bring back some of those?"

"If they are ripe. That reminds me . . . The tribes there like our pottery bowls and our ground corn. If you're not too busy to get some ready, I could trade them for many things. An ornament for your dress. Beads for little Shell Flower. A quiver decorated with porcupine quills to hold Little Otter's arrows."

"I will start on them tomorrow. And I will make a special charm for you, a charm to wear about your neck. With the priest-chief's blessing, it will protect you from evil spirits or witches that might be lurking about."

"Good. One cannot be too careful, especially away from our own country."

They talked on in the darkening night. But Little Otter rolled up in his blanket and tried not to listen.

What does it matter to me? he thought. Not as much as a blue jay's caw. Why can Gray Squirrel go and not this one? I don't understand. What did Father mean, to think like a man? If Leaping Deer were here, he would let me go. Or would he? Anyway, I have Willow. But how exciting a buffalo hunt would be! To see so many new things and places. That Gray Squirrel! He'll strut around like a clown dancer. Why, why can't I go?

Angry and puzzled, the tired boy finally drifted off to sleep.

Later, Pine Tip looked down at his son.

"He grows tall and thin," Pine Tip said to Blue Corn. "What a disappointment for him not to go on the buffalo hunt! But he is still a child in many ways. A good hunter, though, for small creatures. While I am gone, he will supply you with meat. And next year, surely . . ."

Blue Corn bent and pulled the blanket over Little Otter's bare shoulder. "Lately he is happier. Taking care of the coyote was good for him." She smiled. "The tricks, at least, have stopped. He has been too busy."

"I am relieved about one thing," Pine Tip said. "To have that pesky animal gone. A coyote who is not afraid of man! That is trouble! And yet, I could not refuse to fix her leg. For the first time since Leaping Deer died, Little Otter asked my help. I was glad. Do you think he is letting go of Leaping Deer in his mind? Although I try, it is hard even for me. Harder yet for Little Otter, I'm sure."

"Yes. But until Leaping Deer is set free, he cannot join the ancients."

"He loved Little Otter. If he were worried about our son, Leaping Deer would not want to go. I worry too. I hope Little Otter will understand about the buffalo hunt."

Pine Tip rolled up in his blanket. In a few minutes he was snoring softly. Blue Corn, however, sat and

stared into the glowing coals of the fire until they fell
to gray ash. She hugged her shoulders as the chill night
breeze slid in over the doorsill. The buffalo herds were
far away beyond the eastern mountains. Who knew
what dangers were there, what strange gods ruled in
that distant land? She could not keep from worrying.

During the days that followed, Little Otter spent
more time than usual with Willow. His parents were
occupied from early morning until long after sunset
with preparations for the buffalo hunt. Blue Corn
worked many hours making clay jugs and bowls, paint-
ing them, polishing them and firing them under a pile
of hot-burning juniper branches. In the evenings, Pine
Tip beat the drum and sang the grinding song while
Blue Corn rubbed the hard, dried kernels of corn into
meal upon her flat milling stones in the corner of the
room. She also made several sturdy pairs of woven
yucca sandals for her husband, who would need them
to replace those that wore out on the trail.

Pine Tip too was busy. He made a new bow of mes-
quite wood and decorated it with painted designs of
hunters and animals. He made many arrows, carefully
fitting the shafts with bright-colored feathers and perfectly chipped stone points. He would also carry with
him spearheads. Later he would tie them to shafts he
would find in the buffalo country.

One evening while Pine Tip was in the kiva, Little
Otter sang the grinding song for his mother. Soon he
grew tired of the same words over and over. He made
up new ones of his own. Blue Corn looked up in surprise, but she did not stop her rhythmic rubbing of
stone on stone. Then Little Otter began to improvise
a tune and to vary the drumbeat a little to match the
new song.

Blue Corn laughed. "I like it. It is easy to grind corn to that. Is it one you learned from the men in the training classes in . . . ?"

"Stop!" Pine Tip stepped through the doorway and called again, "Stop!"

Little Otter had never heard that sharp note in his father's voice before. Blue Corn put down her grinding stone and rocked back on her heels, startled and frightened. Little Otter sat with mouth open, hands raised above the drum. Was that fear on his father's face also?

Pine Tip snatched the drum. "The corn in the fields is late. No rain comes. Now, this new song! How could you do such a thing? Why do you risk even our scanty store of dried corn? What a disaster if it should spoil!"

"But Father, how could only a song hurt the corn?"

"Don't question the wisdom of the ancient ones. They learned the music best liked by the gods. A different song might also please them. But it might anger them instead. We can't take the chance. I will sing from now on."

Little Otter thought uneasily, Maybe something *will* happen to the corn. If it does, it will be my fault. Why does everything I do seem wrong?

After that, he avoided the village as much as he could. He preferred not to see all the preparations. A few of the boys, including a gradually bolder Gray Squirrel, were annoying in their self-importance as they got ready to accompany the men. Their boasting and their pitying looks were as painful to Little Otter as the sting of a wasp.

One bright afternoon, he was returning from a few hours' hunting down by the river. Over his shoulder he carried a small green-headed duck, the only game he

had found. Gray Squirrel and two companions saw him
climb to the mesa. They waited for him near the corner
of one of the community houses. Because there were
others around, the three troublemakers were limited to
lounging back against the rough stone wall and making
comments.

"Look at the mighty hunter!"

"Strong, too," Gray Squirrel added. "He had to be,
to catch that huge bird."

"If he fights ducks often," said the third, "he'll be
ready to face the fierce buffalo when he is a big boy."
He flapped his arms.

Gray Squirrel joined in with a raucous quacking.
Little Otter didn't answer. He stalked past his tormen-
tors, his face flushed with anger. Their jeering laughs
and the sound of their quacking followed him across
the square.

The teasing was bad enough—but even more important, his pride was injured. He was cut off from a vital
and exciting part of village life. And worst of all, he
had an uncertain feeling that his not being included
might somehow turn out to be mostly his own fault.

Willow was his only comfort. The golden coyote was
now so tame that sometimes he forgot she had ever been
wild.

During these late-summer days, game became harder
to find. The long spell of dry, hot, rainless weather had
driven many wild creatures from the mesas up into the
cooler mountain forests or down into the few canyons
where streams still flowed. Day after day, clouds piled
up in snowy billows over the western mountains; but
in spite of rain dances and special ceremonies, the gods
looked the other way and did not send the needed rain.

Willow's ribs began to show through her bright coat.
She had to hunt both night and day, roaming over a

wide area, to find enough to eat. As far as Little Otter knew, though, she obeyed his command to stay away from the village and its fields.

"The ears of corn grow," he told her. "The squash and beans begin to ripen. Children guard the fields by day, but at night the men take turns. If they see you, they will shoot. To have an arrow in your side, or to have the corn eaten—either would be very bad. So stay away from the fields!" And the coyote seemed to understand.

Little Otter himself was able to kill only an occasional rock squirrel or prairie dog to give a taste of meat to Blue Corn's stews. The poor luck in hunting added to his dissatisfaction, and perhaps this made him careless. Or maybe it wasn't carelessness, but a warning from the gods. Afterward, he couldn't decide which.

It was late afternoon, two days before the men were to go into the kivas for the four days of ritual needed before the buffalo dances could be properly performed. Little Otter had to walk past a group of four or five boys who were huddled together looking at something Gray Squirrel held in his hand. Gray Squirrel was saying, "Deep Lake himself asked me to bring these to the kiva before dawn tomorrow. Just think, maybe we'll be allowed to help fix the buffalo masks. . . ."

And then, as he noticed Little Otter, he put his hand behind his back and said in a loud whisper, "Hush! We mustn't let the children see or hear!"

Little Otter pretended not to notice, but he bit his lip in anger. Why were they so excited about a couple of lightning stones? He had seen them many times. This was just Gray Squirrel's way of making him feel childish and left out. It was not until he joined Willow that he calmed down.

A little later, he was racing Willow along the dry

bed of an arroyo. Then he skidded to a halt as he saw a big pack rat scurry into a juniper thicket.

"Here, Willow! Help me catch him!"

The coyote trotted back. Little Otter parted the branches and peered into the shady interior of the shrubs. Nearby he heard the whirring of a locust.

At that moment, Willow hit him with her shoulder, knocking him sidewise. He rolled over and bounded to his feet.

"Willow! You're crazy! This is not the time for . . ."

Then he saw the thick rattlesnake recoiling beside a bush only a bow's length from where he had been standing. Diamond markings rippled on its long body. It lifted its tail. Again that buzzing rasped the air.

"A locust! How stupid I am!" Little Otter backed slowly away.

Willow, however, faced the deadly serpent. She leaned forward, legs stiff, head down, eyes intent.

Even as Little Otter shouted a warning, the snake struck. Willow jumped high, straight up in the air. The snake's flat head, fangs dripping, passed harmlessly beneath her. Willow came down on top of the writhing body, crunching her teeth into the spine just behind the head.

Little Otter grabbed a rock, but there was no need to throw it. Willow shook the snake vigorously. It was wasted effort. The snake had been dead from the first snap of the coyote's jaws.

Little Otter took the snake from her. He threw his arms around her neck. "It almost bit me. I didn't see it at all. You're brave and smart. But leave it for now. The mate must be close by. If we find it, we'll have one apiece."

Reluctantly, Willow left her kill. Within minutes

they discovered the other rattler, stretched out in the shade of a rock. Willow quickly dispatched it.

"This one is for you," the boy said. Willow settled down to devour it.

Little Otter went back to look at the first snake. It was very long and almost as big around as his arm. The only marks of battle it bore were tooth marks behind the head.

Little Otter's eyes began to glisten with mischief. He had an idea where he could put that snake where it would scare Gray Squirrel and pay him back for his mean remarks. Let's see, he thought, if I take it to the kiva tonight . . .

It was almost dark in the village. The waning moon, showing faintly through the clouds, hung low in the sky as old Red Hawk slowly mounted the ladder from his room to the roof. For half of each year Red Hawk, the head of the Squash, or Summer, people, presided over the village. For the other half of the year Elk, the leader of the Turquoise, or Winter, people governed.

Now the old one stood on the flat roof and looked out over the peaceful square. Patches of orange light from cooking fires inside the homes flickered through ceiling openings and doorways. He saw a late-roaming boy run past on his way home. Little Otter, he thought absently. His mind was occupied with the plans for the cleansing ceremonies that had to be performed before the dances.

Making a decision, Red Hawk descended his ladder. He went to a special niche built into one wall of his room. From it, he lifted a long, very old box, hollowed out of a cottonwood limb.

"These sacred feathers, I take them to the kiva now,"

he told his wife. "Tomorrow there is much to do, many things to prepare for the men."

Laboriously he climbed again to the roof and down another ladder to the ground. With stiff steps, he walked toward a kiva behind the village. Deep shadows hid its drum-shaped outline, but the priest-chief's feet knew the path so well he needed no pine torch.

"Nights," he muttered to himself, "even summer ones. The chill hits the bone. These tired joints hurt."

He held the box carefully, for it contained the feathers to adorn the ceremonial costumes. Tomorrow, after a special ritual, new ones would be added—turkey and eagle feathers with great power, plucked in a certain way from the captive birds. It was most important to do all things correctly to obtain the blessings of the gods so that the hunt would go well and so the whole town would prosper.

Rung by rung, Red Hawk pulled himself up the kiva's outside ladder, holding on with one hand and carrying the box under the other arm. His head rose even with the round, flat roof. Then his breath left him in a sudden, sharp hiss.

"Uff!"

For an awful moment he hung, unable to move, paralyzed with fright. Directly before his eyes was a coiled snake, head raised to strike! Red Hawk stared at the thick, deadly silhouette against the starlit sky.

"Aiii!" he screamed.

He ducked. His hand slipped. He reeled back, missed his footing and flung his other arm wide. The box crashed to the ground. Red Hawk, falling heavily, felt the wood splinter beneath him as he landed upon it.

Hearing the shriek, a man lounging on a nearby roof jumped down to investigate. Peering through the dark, he heard Red Hawk's sorrowful moans. He ran to the priest-chief's side. The old man rolled over painfully and sat up.

"Are you hurt, old one? What happened?"

"I'm not hurt, Round Stone, just shaken. But up there on the roof! It's a snake! And the sacred feathers are here on the ground. They are covered with dust. Now they must all be replaced. What a loss! What a calamity!" And he began to moan again.

By now it was full night. Round Stone got a burning stick from his fireplace and cautiously mounted the ladder to the kiva roof. Red Hawk was right. The snake was still coiled near the head of the ladder. With lightning speed, the man thrust forward the flaming brand. He watched in amazement as the snake collapsed into a lifeless sprawl.

Warily he bent over it. Then he picked it up and tossed it over the edge to the ground.

"Dead! It was dead all the time, old man. Someone thought it would be a joke to put it there. What a joke!"

With foreboding in their hearts, the two men knelt to gather up the bedraggled feathers. Red Hawk's hands felt about in the dirt, but already his mind was busy with the problem.

"We must be especially careful, Round Stone, in the kivas tomorrow—in the preparations, in the dances. This is a bad omen, a poor beginning for the hunt. We must try to undo some of the evil."

the chieftain-bird

Morning, however, brought more trouble.

Blue Corn woke early. She was kneading clay for a bowl when she heard excited voices and running footsteps. She went to the doorway and leaned out.

"What is it? What happens?"

The first woman to pass was her neighbor, Brown Bird. She looked at Blue Corn and then bustled by without answering. Blue Corn's fingers squeezed the lump of clay so hard it tore into two pieces. She slapped them back together. Brown Bird had never spoken to her in all the years they had lived right next to each other. Would she ever get used to such treatment?

Then Squash Blossom came hurrying across the square. As Blue Corn went to meet her, she thought, Only something important would make Squash Blossom move that fast.

Squash Blossom twisted the end of her braided belt. "The turkey pens," she said breathlessly. "That is all I heard. Something bad has happened. I feel it."

"Then this one will stay here."

"It is safer so. They might think a foreigner . . . I go to find out. When I know, I will come to tell you."

Little Otter rolled over, heard the commotion, and raced to see what was going on, rubbing sleep from his eyes as he ran. Pine Tip refused to be hurried.

"I will eat now. Bad news can take away a man's appetite."

Blue Corn had to laugh at his wry smile.

Dogs, infected by the excitement, barked and fought among themselves. Little Otter almost fell over one of them. He stopped in his tracks. The dog was playing with a dead rattlesnake. He recognized the marks behind the head.

"Oh!" He kicked at the dog. "You've spoiled everything! I had it set up just right. Now Gray Squirrel . . ." He shrugged his shoulders. "It's too late now. Already there is too much light to put it back. And it was such a good trick, too." He ran on.

At the turkey pens a circle of people stood silently, patiently. Some of the women held their hands over their mouths. Only their frightened dark eyes showed. The square faces of the men were stern and set, looking as though they had been carved from red-brown rock. Little Otter inched his way between and around the broad bodies, trying to see. Frustrated, he got down and crawled through a mass of legs until he reached the front. He stared unbelievingly. He gasped, and his jaw dropped. Then he sat down with a bump.

"The chieftain-bird!"

The old eagle was gone! The sides of the wooden cage were broken. The perch was empty. He jerked his head around. Thank the gods, he thought. The turkeys, at least, were all right.

He rubbed his head until his hair stuck out in all directions like the stiff leaves of the yucca plant. He wanted to question someone, but he knew he would have to wait like the others.

At last Red Hawk scuffed slowly down the path. "What has happened here?"

The crowd parted to let him through. When he saw

the cage, he stopped. Then, moving as if in a dream, the old man stumbled up to it. He stared in shocked disbelief at the empty perch.

"The chieftain-bird!" His voice sounded like the croak of a raven. His fingers groped for his necklace of bear's teeth. "Who? What?"

Round Stone and another man came forward. "It was a coyote, old one. We found tracks in the dust. Patches of hair were on the broken pieces of the cage."

Round Stone added, "The eagle was tethered, and old. It must have been easy. How I would like to kill that coyote! It dragged the chieftain-bird over to the cliff edge. There we found what was left."

The other man said, "I was guarding the fields last night. A coyote came. It showed no fear. But when I raised my bow and arrow to shoot, it ran. I could not tell whether I hit it or not. Deep Lake and I chased it. But Deep Lake fell over a rock. He lies now with a back that hurts and will not let him walk. I stopped to help him, and the coyote got away. Maybe it came up onto the mesa after that."

Little Otter looked from one speaker to the other. He bit his lip hard. His stomach began to churn. Coyote! He scuttled back through the wilderness of legs. Once away from the crowd, he began to run.

It could not be, he thought. No, Willow wouldn't do such a thing! But he had to find out. If it *had* been Willow, what if she were hurt? He stumbled down the paths and stepped on cactus plants, but he felt no pain. As he ran, it seemed as though the bars of a cage were closing in about him too.

Later he could not remember getting to Willow's den, but he would never forget the bloody feathers he saw strewn around the entrance. It was too much for him to take in all at once. He slumped onto a rock. Head in hands, he groaned.

"What shall I do? Willow, Willow, how could you! What can I do?"

When he started back to the village, he walked haltingly, painfully. Slowly he climbed up the stairs through the cleft. At the top, Pine Tip was waiting for him.

"Father! I must talk to . . ."

Pine Tip stopped him with an upheld hand. "Come to the flat rocks. Then you can tell me."

Solemnly they went down the hill, past the turkey pens and the ruined eagle cage, through a field of squash and beans, to the rocks. Pine Tip motioned for Little Otter to sit.

"Now."

Little Otter could not look at his father. He gazed with unseeing eyes toward the valley of the great river. "I didn't tell you all. The coyote *was* free. But she stayed near. She wanted to, and I let her. We hunt and play together each day. She's my friend. I didn't think . . ." His voice broke and he could not go on.

"You didn't think she would kill the eagle—the chieftain-bird that gives us feathers for our dances, feathers to carry our prayers safely to the gods."

Little Otter nodded, his hands over his eyes. Then he looked up in surprise. "How did you know?"

Pine Tip held up a fluff of golden fur. "This. It was on the bars of the cage. If you had given her no reason to stay, the coyote would have gone to the mountains where there is more game, or to the river valley. But near the village! Trouble had to come. Now you know. The whole town suffers because of it. If only you had sent her away! Where is she?"

"Hunting. Sleeping somewhere, maybe. I went to her den. She isn't there. But there were feathers, blood, part of an eagle wing. She didn't know! Truly, Father! She's just a coyote. How could she know what it would mean to us?"

"The dances. Without the chieftain-bird's feathers, we cannot hold them when we planned. To wait is to get back from the hunt too late for harvest. After harvest, the winter comes too soon to give us time to hunt for buffalo.

"One thing this must teach you. Only one, if nothing else. Each happening affects us all, even when we think it is a private affair."

"But Red Hawk, does he not have more feathers? In the special box?"

Pine Tip looked sorrowfully at his son. There was a long silence. Little Otter felt a chill creep down his spine. Finally his father spoke.

"The old one took the box to the kiva last evening. It was dark. A rattlesnake was coiled at the top of the ladder. How could Red Hawk know it was dead? He fell. The box broke. Many feathers are torn. All are soiled with dust."

"Oh, Ohhh, no! Father, I . . ." Little Otter choked back a sob. "That's my fault too. I heard Gray Squirrel say he was going there early this morning. I wanted to play a joke on him, a trick. All of it is my fault."

"No, the fault is mine too. What you do is my responsibility until you are a man. Come. We must talk with Red Hawk."

Little Otter was more wounded by his father's quiet acceptance of equal guilt than he would have been by his anger. They walked in silence. In silence, too, the old priest-chief listened to Little Otter's confession. Then he said, "It is of no use to wish these things undone. But to dance we must have eagle feathers, feathers obtained in the proper way from an unharmed bird. It will be a hard winter. The hunt, it *must* be successful. We need the chieftain-bird. Only he can help us."

"If only we could catch another," Pine Tip said. "But I've seen no eagles this whole summer."

"Nor I." Red Hawk shook his head in despair. His fingers plucked constantly at his necklace.

"I have!"

They both turned to Little Otter.

"I saw one! I can show you where."

They stared at him. He nodded, his eyes bright with excitement. Then they looked at each other. Their shoulders straightened.

"We must try," Pine Tip said. "Come, my son."

"This old one will make prayer sticks for you. Other things, too, to win favor from the gods. Perhaps they will give us another chance."

"Little Otter, you must find some bait," Pine Tip said as they hurried across the square. "A jackrabbit or a marmot—something about that size. Quickly! We have this afternoon, and that is all."

"You eat first," Blue Corn insisted, when Little Otter ran inside for his hunting gear and was about to rush right out. "With a full stomach you will hunt better."

The morning sun reflected from the cliffs and dazzled Little Otter's eyes as he climbed the trail to the higher mesas. With every step, he asked the gods to forgive him for the mistakes he had made.

There is just one way I can mend things, he thought. We must catch an eagle!

Back and forth across the upper mesas he ranged, skirting the fields belonging to the other village, the one in the canyon below. Its men also were going on the buffalo hunt. He wondered if they were getting ready for their dances. They must be, he decided, for the women were working in the fields instead of the men. They were carrying water to the rows of corn.

Nearby a mother called to her young son—a thin, wiry boy of six or seven years, who was pulling out weeds from around the plants. "Quick Jay! Quick Jay, your father wants feathers for his arrows. Tomorrow you can take your net to the small mountain. Perhaps you can catch a yellow warbler or a bluebird."

"Oh yes, Mother!" The boy gave a few hops of joy at the prospect of a day in the woods. Then he bent again to his weeding.

At the end of an hour, Little Otter was discouraged. For a moment he wished Willow were with him. She would have found something before this. He had seen only small birds, a field mouse or two and one cottontail rabbit that had darted away before he had a chance to lift his throwing stick. He had found no game worthy of an eagle. But this was one day he hoped Willow would stay far away from him. She did not belong on an eagle hunt.

Then, as he stealthily approached a tangle of juniper and oak, there was a rustle in the dead leaves of the year before. He froze, his throwing stick in his upraised hand. A faint clucking made his heart beat faster. Brush crackled, and a fat grouse, dignified and slow, strutted out into the open.

Little Otter's arm flashed. The curved stick flew to its target. The grouse fell dead before it could spread its wings for flight. With a cry of triumph, Little Otter pounced upon it. He lifted it to his shoulder and started back down the trail.

When Little Otter appeared, Pine Tip had a neat pack ready. It contained a large net made of yucca cording, a length of dark cotton cloth, a square of soft weasel skin, rawhide lacings and one of Blue Corn's flat bowls. In addition, he carried a throwing stick, in case he should see game, an ax and his sharp obsidian knife.

Father and son took their burdens to the house of Red Hawk. There the old man sang a special chant for their success, blessed them and presented them with prayer sticks topped with downy white feathers. In addition, he gave Pine Tip a good-luck stone to wear on his turquoise necklace and a little pouch of sacred meal to sprinkle on and around the bait.

"I go to the kiva now to pray that the chieftain-bird will give himself to you," he said. "May the gods smile on us and fill our needs."

Little Otter led the way south across the canyons and mesas to the place where he had seen the eagle. Neither he nor his father noticed the golden coyote who raced across the brush-covered flats to meet Little Otter. Nor did they see that Willow, upon finding the boy accompanied by another human, settled back to follow at a safe distance.

AN EAGLE TRAP

"There's the dead tree," Little Otter said. "I think the eagle's nest is below, on the face of the cliff."

Pine Tip shaded his eyes and searched the sky. Then he pointed. Little Otter had to look hard to make out the tiny dark speck far overhead.

"He hunts," Pine Tip said. "We will prepare a meal for him."

He walked along the mesa until he found a place suitable to his purpose. The bedrock here was split into several deep fissures wide enough for a man to hide in without being seen above the level of the ground. He laid down his pack.

"Here, my son. Fill this bowl at the stream in the bottom of the canyon. Don't spill the water while you're climbing back up. Go now. I'll fix the trap."

Little Otter skirted the rim of the mesa until he reached a pile of rubble over which he could scramble down into the canyon. At the bottom, he pushed through a fringe of alders and wild roses to the bank of the stream. A woodpecker hammered on a tree trunk overhead. Bees swarmed around a berry bush. Little Otter bent to fill the bowl.

Suddenly a soft whine sounded in his ear. A nudge against his ribs almost sent him sprawling. He caught his balance and gently set the bowl down in the grass.

"Willow! You crazy coyote! Where did you come from? What if I had broken the bowl?"

The coyote panted happily, her head cocked, her tongue lolling out. He dropped to his knees beside her.

"How could you kill the chieftain-bird? Don't you know what trouble you caused?" He considered a moment, then added, "Of course, it was mostly my fault. I let you stay. I put the snake on the kiva. Because of us, you and me, it is necessary to try to catch another eagle."

He drew in his breath sharply. "Oh, the eagle! You must go away! You *can't* stay here. It's bad enough now. How much worse it will be if you stay! The eagle won't come down. Or if he does, you might hurt him after he's caught. Then the feathers couldn't be used. Willow, you must leave. Go!" He jumped up. Stamping his foot, he pointed down the canyon. "Go home! Go to your den!"

Willow backed away. She was puzzled. Was this a new game? Her yellow eyes became eager. She dashed back and forth, ready to romp. Her ears twitched.

"Willow, go!"

She tilted her head, watching, looking for a sign she could understand.

Little Otter was near despair. He picked up a few pebbles and threw them at her feet. Willow backed away, bewildered.

"Please! Please, go!" Little Otter choked at the hurt look in her eyes. "You *have* to!" He threw a larger stone. It struck the coyote's long, sensitive nose. With a yelp, she whirled and slunk out of sight in the underbrush.

Little Otter hugged his stomach. His throat hurt. How he wished he could call her back! He lay down by the stream and drank. The water felt cool on his lips and hands and on his hot, dusty face. But the lump in his throat wouldn't go away.

I had to do it, he told himself. Now I must hurry. There are important things to do, important for all of us in the village. I must think of them.

Carefully carrying the bowlful of water, he slowly climbed up to the mesa. His father had the trap nearly ready. Across one of the fissures in the rock he had laid a row of pine branches. The strong center poles were concealed with piñon boughs and weighted on either side with heavy stones. There was room within the broken rock for a man to crouch under the poles.

"Why do you want the bowl of water, Father?"

"To put on the ground inside the trap. In it, I can see the reflection of the eagle when he circles and comes lower. When he alights, I will act quickly."

"But how will you catch him without hurting him?"

"He must perch here to get the bait." Pine Tip pointed to the heavy center poles. "When he does, I'll reach up through the branches and grasp his legs. These thongs are to tie him to the poles. And you will help, too."

"How?"

"You must lie quietly in the crack in the rock over there. Stay under the branches and do not make a sound. Listen for my call. When you hear it, you must jump up and throw this net over the eagle. He must not hurt his wings by beating them about. Then, over the net spread the cloth. With his head in the dark, he'll be still."

Little Otter scratched one leg with the toes of the

other foot. "He is a very big bird. I hope it works." He sounded doubtful.

"I too. Much depends upon it. We are ready. I will ask the gods to help us."

Pine Tip took the small prayer sticks that Red Hawk had given him. He placed them carefully about the pit to the north, south, east and west. Each time he pushed one into the ground, he chanted a plea for success. The downy feathers topping the sticks would hurry the prayers to the sky gods and to the chieftain-bird wheeling above.

Then Pine Tip tied the grouse firmly to the poles above the trap. On the bait and on the ground around it he sprinkled sacred cornmeal, singing more prayers as he did so. When the ritual was over, he lifted his head and scanned the heavens, as blue as the finest tur-quoise in his necklace.

"He has heard! He's coming! Run to your hiding place. When I call, throw the net quickly."

Little Otter lay in the crack in the rock and tried to catch sight of the circling eagle through the openings between the branches. Sometimes he could see it clearly. Then for long minutes of almost unbearable suspense the patch of sky was empty. Whenever the eagle reappeared, it was larger and lower than the time before.

"He has seen the bait. He comes closer," Little Otter whispered.

His lungs were heavy with the spicy scent of the sun-warmed boughs. His mouth was dry with excitement and the heat of the dusty crevice. The throbbing of his pulse filled his ears. Surely the chieftain-bird would hear its pounding and stay away.

But no, he was coming!

This time the bird was so low that Little Otter almost cried out. With its great wings spread wide, the eagle swept over his hiding place. The boughs stirred with the wind of its passage. Loosened sand trickled down the rock and over Little Otter's shoulder.

Afraid to move, he waited. Would his father be able to grasp those legs armed with terrible talons? He listened, straining, palms wet with sweat. Why didn't something happen? How long would they have to . . . ?

All at once there was a furious flapping. A shout.

"Little Otter! The net!"

The boy scrambled out of the crack and grabbed up the net. He held it wide and ran to the pit.

Face to face with the eagle, he stopped. His arms refused to move. He could only stand and stare. Never had he seen such power, such anger in a living creature! The wicked curved beak was open, ugly, yellow. Horrible cackling burst from it. Huge wings spread wider than a man is tall. Their frantic flapping raised a cloud of dust through which yellow eyes glared at him.

"Little Otter! Hurry!"

Pine Tip's call broke the spell. With a swift throw, the boy covered the outraged chieftain-bird with the net. Quickly he rolled stones onto the edges to hold it down. Then he tossed the cloth over the net to cover the eagle.

"It is done! I did it, Father!"

The eagle gabbled so loudly that Pine Tip didn't hear his son's words. But the cloth, darkening the pit, told him all was well. He breathed easier. Carefully, uttering a soft prayer, he eased a leather thong about one of the bird's legs, holding tightly all the while to the other leg. The hard part was just beginning.

Up above, Little Otter bent to place another stone

on the net. At that moment, a tremendous shadow blotted out the sun and darkened the ground around him. He felt a rush of wind. An awesome beating shook the air. He looked up. His hands flew up to guard his face. His eyes glazed with fear.

The words screamed in his head. Father! Help! Another eagle! But no sound came from his throat. He turned and ran for his life.

The captive eagle's mate swept so low over Little Otter that one dark wing struck his head. He stumbled and almost fell. Curved talons reached out for him. Yellow eyes gleamed so close that he saw the pits on either side of the open, hissing beak.

"Father! The mate!" he shrieked. "Help me!"

But Pine Tip, deep within the rock, did not hear.

Shielding his head with his arms, Little Otter ran like a frightened rabbit, darting first one way, then another. The enraged bird followed. It wheeled and swooped, skimming the bushes. The sun glinted on its snowy head and tail. A patch of scrub oak loomed ahead. If only he could get into it! There he would be safe.

He jumped over a log, tripped on a branch and fell hard. Gasping, he tried to pull air into his lungs. The eagle sailed down, talons spread. Little Otter rolled into a ball. His eyes closed tight, and his muscles tensed. In his imagination he already felt the tearing claws. Wind from the wings stirred his hair, and he heard the bird's harsh cry. But at the last moment, the eagle flew upward. Why had it not struck?

Then he heard a volley of barking. He sat up as a golden streak flashed past. Willow! It was Willow who had frightened the bird away. But now it returned. Coyote and eagle rushed to meet. Willow leaped high, snapping. The eagle wheeled away, blood staining its

tail. Again and again Willow jumped, until her quarry flew off over the treetops. Little Otter ran to his pet.

"Willow, you chased it away. Brave coyote! Oh, but it hurt you." He reached to touch the crimson streaks across one bright shoulder. Then he ducked as once again a shadow slid across the earth toward them.

"Watch out, Willow! It's coming back!" Little Otter dived into the middle of the oak thicket, for once thankful for the prickly branches. "Come here! Hurry!"

But the coyote turned to do battle once more. She snapped and jumped so viciously that the eagle was forced to swerve away. This time it mounted high into the sky and circled, ever watchful.

Pine Tip, busy securing the other eagle, had neither seen nor heard the fight above. When he had finished tying the captured bird to the sturdy center poles, he climbed out onto the mesa. In front of him was the coyote, sitting on her haunches, trying to lick her bloody shoulder. Pine Tip stared.

"That coyote again! Look at her! She has hurt our eagle. I'll kill her. She won't trouble us again."

Pine Tip ran for his stone ax, but Little Otter sprang from the thicket and threw his arms around Willow's neck.

"No! No, Father! She saved me. She drove away the other eagle. The one we caught is safe. Look at it. Please, Father!"

Slowly Pine Tip lowered his arm. He examined the tethered bird. Then he dropped the ax.

"What do you mean, the other eagle?"

The boy pointed to the mate, soaring high above. "It came after me. I fell. Willow chased it. She was just in time. It almost got me. Now Willow is hurt."

Pine Tip watched the coyote for a moment. He looked at Little Otter's pleading face. Then he walked over to the pit, cut loose the remains of the fat grouse and dropped it under Willow's nose.

"Here—a just reward for saving my son."

Willow wasted no time. She crouched and began tearing at the bird. Little Otter grinned. He whispered into one black-tipped ear.

"If you are very good, maybe you can stay after all."

The next morning Little Otter stood alone, apart from the women and children who watched as the men met in the square before filing into the kivas to begin their careful four-day rituals and preparations for the buffalo dances. When Gray Squirrel joined the men, Little Otter clenched his teeth. He kept his face stiff and expressionless.

"Too bad you won't be with us," Gray Squirrel called. "Maybe next year you'll be big enough."

Little Otter's eyes glittered with anger, but he said nothing. He lifted his chin. No one would see that it mattered. He would be glad when the men were all in the kivas. Then he and Willow would go off by themselves. His father had said nothing about the coyote. Surely that meant she could remain. After all, she had saved his life. That ought to be reason enough to let her stay.

Just then Pine Tip stepped from their doorway and came across the square to speak to him. He placed his hand on Little Otter's shoulder.

"I'm sorry, my son. Soon, though, you will take your place with us."

Little Otter nodded. No words could tell how he felt. Pine Tip looked at him from under straight black brows, and said, "The coyote, we have not spoken of her. You know, of course, she cannot stay. In spite of her help and bravery, she must go. The welfare of the

whole town is more important than one coyote. Take
her far away, or I will kill her. It is not what I want to
do, but it is a necessity. Today you must decide. She is
like a child. She does not understand, just as you said.
You must think for her. One way or another, she has
to go. She doesn't belong here."

He waited for an answer, but Little Otter's throat
was so full he couldn't speak. After a moment, Pine
Tip walked across to the other men. One by one, they
climbed the ladders into the kivas.

Little Otter stood with his head bent. A horned toad
scuttled by, making a funny little trail in the dust. The
boy stared at it without seeing it. Neither did he see
the people who stepped out of his way as he crossed the
square to his home.

In the darkest corner of the room, he sat down on the
floor and leaned against the wall. The mud plaster felt
smooth and cool on his bare back. Shell Flower, in her
hanging cradleboard, slept peacefully. Little Otter's
thoughts went round and round. He must take Willow
away. She could not stay here. She didn't belong. His
father would kill her. What to do? Chewing at his
thumb, he pondered the question. Surely if he thought
long and hard enough, he could find an answer.

Suddenly he banged his fist against the clay floor. "If
Willow doesn't belong, neither do I. I'll take her far
away, as Father told me to do. But I won't leave her.
We'll go together."

My mother's village! he thought. I can go there! My
uncles, they will take me in, make me welcome. I will
be a member of the great Antelope clan. Who knows?
In time I might even become chief like my grandfather.

Now he was fiercely glad that he had not been initiated into his father's society in this village. Surely he
would feel more at home in the western town where

his mother had been born. How exciting life would be there! He was surprised he hadn't thought of it before. He would belong there as he had never belonged here on the mesa. He had always known he was different from the other boys. Now he was glad of it. Here he had been lonely. There he would have more friends than he had thought possible. Before he left, though, he must learn more about the length and difficulty of the journey.

When Blue Corn entered the doorway a few minutes later, she found Little Otter still sitting, his eyes shining with excitement. She put down her brimming water jar.

"It is good you are not sulking about the hunt. Or the coyote either. You are growing up." She unlaced the cradleboard and lifted Shell Flower out. The baby gurgled happily.

"I need a pair of sandals, Mother. Will you have time today to make them? It will take a day and a half to get so far away that Willow won't come back to the plateau. I'll need sandals."

"Oh? Until now, you fussed about wearing them even in winter. But if you want them . . . Yes, I have strips left from your father's."

"This morning," Little Otter said, "I'll work in the fields. Then I'll hunt. This afternoon when you're making the sandals, perhaps you'll tell me stories of your home? The one in the western country?"

Blue Corn smiled. But she looked after him thoughtfully when he left. She had expected storm clouds. Instead, there was sunshine. It was puzzling.

At high noon, the boy returned with a marmot. He skinned it while Blue Corn took a basket of fragrant corn cakes to the kiva for the men, who would eat and sleep there until the dances were over. Then Blue

Corn's nimble fingers plaited and wove strips of yucca leaves into sandals while she told Little Otter of her life before she had come to the village on the mesa. She spoke of customs among her people, of visitors, of travelers passing through her town on their way to the salt lakes. She described the fierce Navajos and Apaches, who were rarely seen on this side of the mountains. Sometimes, she said, they only wanted to trade, and when they came in peace they were welcomed. But at other times they raided the fields and even stole women or children. She told about an aunt who had been a captive of the Navajos for many years.

"When she escaped at last and returned to our village, she spent long days in weeping."

"She was sad? Why?"

"About only one thing. It almost stopped her heart to leave her children, the ones of her Navajo husband. Often she worried and wondered about them. She said her husband was like many Navajo men. They learn our language from their stolen wives so that they can make better trades in our villages. How terrible it would be to be stolen away by one of them!"

Little Otter questioned her about the route across the mountains. She remembered it well.

"It was a fine journey. My brothers showed us the trail. Sometimes it went by the river; sometimes between steep cliffs, red and orange, very high. Up, up we climbed into the mountains, following the river all the time. Through forests of great pines and spruce trees we went. We saw deer and bears, and once a huge mountain lion.

"At last we reached the round valley nestled among the high peaks. From there, your father knew the way. At sunset we came over the pass. It took my breath away. These mesas and canyons; the great valley with

the river shining golden in the center; the eastern
mountains all pink with their heads in the purple
clouds. When I saw it for the first time that way, it
seemed the gods had given me a very special gift. Never
have I forgotten it."

She finished the sandals and handed them to him.
"Here they are. Take the coyote a long way off. It is
for her good as well as ours. Remember, no traveling
after dark! One should not tempt the evil spirits, the
ghosts and witches, who roam about at night."

She smiled as she went to get Shell Flower. "I'm
glad," she said over her shoulder, "that you will be
here while your father is gone. It is selfish to feel so,
but I need you, especially since your sister is so small.
You're a great help, a fine hunter. Besides, it will not
be so lonesome. Hurry back!"

RAIDERS

Late in the afternoon, high up on the mountainside, Little Otter spoke to the coyote. "A storm comes, Willow. Look at those clouds over the peaks. This time they bring rain for sure. Everybody will be happy. The crops will grow quickly. They'll ripen before frost. But now we must find a dry place to spend the night."

He sat on a flat rock to rest from the constant climbing and to think. Willow, panting, lay beside him. Behind and on either side, the forest was dim and quiet. Birds chirped softly, flitting about in their evening search for food. On a branch just above his head, a hidden solitaire sang, "Weep! Weep! Weep!" over and over.

Little Otter threw an acorn at it. "Go away! Or sing a happier song."

But the solitaire, flying away, was replaced by a sapsucker that mewed sadly, like a lost bobcat kitten. The boy closed his ears with his fingers and looked at the view.

Here and there on the mesas below he could see patches of small green fields. The canyons were chasms running over with darkness. Evening shadows crept out toward the valley of the great river, where the sunlight was still bright. The valley itself and the eastern mountains seemed to float in shimmering red-gold air. It was so clear that Little Otter could see the round drum shape of the small orphan mesa standing all by itself on the other side of the river. On this side he thought he could see the outlines of the community houses of his own village.

For a moment he felt a queer tug at his heart, a dryness in his throat. But his mother's country would be fine too. And he would come back sometimes. Perhaps after the winter was over, he would bring news to her. How happy she would be to know about her family!

A low growl of thunder brought him back to the present.

"Come on, Willow! An old hunting camp is near. I remember a small house there. A good place to get out of the storm. Just above the camp is the pass to the round valley. Tomorrow we'll be on the trail to the flat country."

Quietly, because he was watching for a squirrel or rabbit to catch and cook for dinner, Little Otter slipped through the woods. Willow, also hunting a meal, ran from his side out of sight among the trees. A sudden "Yip! Yip!" halted the boy. He listened. Something had alarmed Willow. What was it?

Then he heard a low mutter of voices from farther up the mountain and smelled a wandering wisp of woodsmoke. Hunters, he thought, but from where? All the men of the two nearer villages were in their kivas preparing for the buffalo dances.

He sneaked silently through the forest, circling around and above the sounds until he stood in the shelter of a thick grove of white-trunked aspens. He looked down into a grassy clearing. He recognized the place. On one side stood the walls and part of the roof of a stone building, all that remained of the old hunting hut. In front of the hut was a crackling campfire, surrounded by a group of brown-skinned men. Their long shadows darted in the firelight. They were big men, strong-looking and tall, with high-bridged noses and coarse black hair bound back from their faces with bright woven bands.

Their faces! Little Otter stared. Their cheekbones and foreheads were streaked with red, white and yellow paint! He drew in his breath. War paint! He shivered violently. Then he backed away. As quickly as he could without making any noise, he climbed the mountain toward the round valley. He wanted to put as much distance as possible between himself and the raiders.

A few minutes later, he stopped. Of course! he thought. That's what they are. They're raiders. I guess I knew it all the time. I just didn't put it into words.

Willow came running back to him. She whined.

"Wait, Willow. I have to think."

He leaned against a tree. She came and sat beside him, then trotted away a few steps and returned. "If they are raiders," he asked her, "where are they going?"

He began to walk again, so swiftly that he was almost running. The coyote bounded ahead. What difference does it make to me where they go? Little Otter thought angrily. My business is to find the trail to my mother's village.

In his mind he saw his mother as he had last seen her, with her black hair cut straight across her forehead and hanging in shining braids down her back. She was smiling and holding Shell Flower. Reluctantly, he slowed down.

"Willow," he said with a sigh, "we go back. I don't

want to, but I must. Do you understand? I *have* to."
He began to retrace his steps.

When he stood again in the grove and looked at the
men in the clearing below, he felt a sickness in his
stomach. He knew he would have to try to find out
their plans, but he was shaking with fright. He had
heard terrible stories of what happened to those who
were taken prisoner by war parties. He made himself
slide inch by inch down the slope until at last he lay
flat under the low, spreading branches of a sheltering
fir tree. There in the dark shadows he felt a little safer.

The men talked openly, unafraid. From his hiding
place the boy tried to hear what they said. After a few
minutes he shook his head in disappointment. They
were using a language he could not understand.

Navajos, he thought. They look just the way Mother
described them. Why have they come? Oh, of course—
to steal our corn! And they don't know the harvest is
later this year than usual.

Pine needles rustled near his feet. Little Otter's
heart gave a painful thump. He twisted his head
around to look. Then he let his breath out silently.
Willow! She crouched close to the ground and crawled
under the branches to his side, sniffing about nervously.
He rested his hand on her head and whispered to her
to lie still.

He could think of nothing better to do, so they
waited while the clouds piled up and the evening shadows turned to blackness. Little Otter began to shake
with the cold, and he tucked his feet under Willow's
warm side.

Below them, the painted strangers strutted about
and spoke loudly. Their lack of caution frightened
Little Otter more than anything else. It showed how

invincible they thought themselves to be. And he was sure they had good reason to feel that way.

As far as he knew, the raiders—he counted eleven of them—might be on their way to one of the distant villages to the north or south. But perhaps they were planning to raid *his* village! If I could only find out, he thought. How, though, when their words are strange? The odor of deer haunches roasting over their fire reminded him pointedly that he had not eaten.

He was about to give up his vigil and slip away into the aspen grove when he heard a shout from one side of the clearing. He rolled over to look. Then he sat up straight, striking his head on a low limb. His muffled exclamation of pain and surprise was unnoticed by the men below as they gathered in a noisy group about the two new arrivals. One was a short, muscular man in war paint; the other, a small boy he hauled along by one arm.

Little Otter frowned as he looked at the youngster's frightened face. Why, he thought, he is the small one from the other village that I saw in the fields on the mesa yesterday. The one who was to look for birds. I can't remember his name. I think it was that of a bird too.

He pictured the mother working in the field and imagined hearing her call to her son. Ah, Quick Jay, he thought. His name is Quick Jay.

The boy's captor, who had a long white scar across his chest, flung the boy down and stood over him, laughing cruelly. He waved his sharp stone knife. The child lay speechless, too terrified to move or make a sound. Another man pushed through the encircling men and spoke to the newcomer.

This one, thought Little Otter, is the leader. He was taller than the others, and heavyset. His nose was pushed to one side, as though it had been broken. "Crooked Nose" asked a question, pointing toward Quick Jay. The captor—Little Otter called him "Scar Chest"—shouted harshly to the child.

In his hiding place, Little Otter jerked to attention. The last words had been spoken in his own language. Again the question was asked, this time accompanied by a rough kick.

"Where is your village?"

The trembling child pointed toward the valley.

Motioning to Willow to stay where she was, Little Otter crept silently from one tree to another until he reached a new hiding place—behind a fallen tree trunk, just out of the firelight. Now, he thought, I can hear very well. They are so busy with Quick Jay, they won't be watching carefully. He strained to hear every word.

The questioning went on, accompanied by an occasional hard cuff of the Navajo's rough hand. "The corn, it is still in the fields. Is it ready to bring in?"

Quick Jay shook his tousled black head. "Not for many days." He ducked a blow and insisted in a shrill voice, "No, it's not ready! Planting was late this year."

When Scar Chest relayed this to the others, a babble broke out. Little Otter's hopes rose. Maybe they would decide to go home. But Crooked Nose quieted them with a motion of his arm. He spoke in grunting phrases to Scar Chest. The latter finally turned to his captive.

"He says there is always ground corn in jars in the houses, and other corn stored for seed. Is this right?"

Quick Jay hesitated. A hard kick landed on his ribs. He gasped, "Yes."

"Where are your men? I saw only women and children as I watched from the cliffs."

"In the kivas."

"Why?"

"Getting ready for dances."

"When?"

The child held up four fingers. "That many days."

"Aha!" The painted face frowned ferociously. "You lie! They do the corn dances. They get ready to bring in the harvest."

"No, no!" Quick Jay stuttered. "I told—I spoke the truth. They prepare for the buffalo dances."

Scar Chest straightened and stared. "Buffalo!" He spoke quickly to the others. Then he turned back to Quick Jay. "Just your village?"

"No. The one on the mesa too."

"And then they go to hunt the buffalo? When?"

The answer was lost in a long roll of thunder. The rain gods are waking, Little Otter thought. He looked up. Black clouds rushed across the sky, blotting out the thin little moon. Lightning flared, and the thunder god rumbled again.

"What did you say?" Scar Chest shouted.

Quick Jay's eyes were wide and white with fear. "Five days."

His captor passed on the information, his words running together. He spread his hands, waving toward the eastern mountains. Crooked Nose nodded. He turned his back on the others and stared at the fire, thinking. Then he pointed to the clearing and gave his orders. The others grinned. They slapped their thighs, delighted with his decision.

Scar Chest looked at Quick Jay. "We stay here until your men leave for the hunt. Then we raid not one, but two villages! We get corn and slaves. And there will be no one to follow, to bother us like flies, on our journey home. Ha! That is good! And you, little puppy, will show us the best way to each village. Or"—he lifted

Quick Jay by an arm—"you do not live to see the harvest! You understand?"

He dragged the boy over to the ruined building and shoved him through the opening. Then Scar Chest sat on the doorsill and chewed on the half-raw chunk of meat that Crooked Nose threw to him.

Little Otter began to back away. Accidentally, he put his hand on a small branch. It cracked under his weight.

Crooked Nose jumped up with an exclamation of alarm. He lifted his hand for silence. While the others watched, he picked up a war club and started across the clearing. Little Otter's face drained. He cowered against the ground as he heard the footsteps come closer and closer. Just then a coyote yipped nearby. Willow! Would she give him away?

But the men by the fire laughed, and one called out to Crooked Nose. He seemed to be saying, "See, it was only a coyote. Come and eat."

The footsteps stopped. Little Otter held his breath. Then he heard Crooked Nose grunt in agreement, and the footsteps receded toward the fire. Little Otter went limp with relief. The ground was damp and cold under his cheek as he silently took a few deep breaths. He waited until the next roll of thunder before he moved.

The noise of the approaching storm covered Little Otter's retreat. He crept back to the fir tree, picked up his pack and whispered for Willow. The two circled wide around the clearing. Willow ran silently beside the boy, who skidded and slid down the mountainside on a carpet of pine needles. Little Otter thanked the thunder god. He could go much faster when he didn't have to worry about being quiet. And he must hurry home to give notice of the coming raid.

Blue Corn, wakeful with both husband and son away, sat up with a small cry as Little Otter climbed through the doorway.

"It's all right, Mother. It is only me."

"Little Otter! Back so soon? Surely you have not had time . . ." She stopped as she saw his face in the glow of the low fire. "But do not speak now. Warm yourself. You are wet and cold." She laid some wood on the coals in the small open hearth.

"I'm hungry, too," Little Otter said.

The beating rain made a muffled drumming on the roof. Little Otter crouched next to the dancing blaze. Only after he had eaten a bowl of marmot stew and had stopped shivering would his mother let him talk.

"We got only as far as the first mountain," he told her. "To the old hunting camp, where we were going to spend the night. But a raiding party was camping there! Navajos, I think, from the other side of the range. They wear war paint! And they are coming here! We must warn the men."

"Navajos! So close! But calm yourself, my son. They do nothing at night. They too fear witches and ghosts. They attack only in daylight."

Little Otter held out his bowl for more stew. Was it only this morning he had killed the marmot he was eating now? It seemed much longer than that. He ate until he was full, warm inside and out. Then he told his mother about his discovery of the raiders, their little captive and what he had heard of their plans. Blue Corn listened, interrupting once in a while to ask a question.

Finally Little Otter said, "And that is all. Shall I go to the kiva now? The men will want to attack the camp."

"No!" Blue Corn spoke so sharply that Little Otter jumped. More quietly she went on, "You say the Navajos wait there. They will not attack until the men leave. We have time, time to think and plan." She frowned, chewing on her lower lip with her small white teeth.

"Our men are brave," she said, "but they are not warriors. They are farmers. I have seen it happen before. When a few men sneak into a raiders' camp, they kill some, but most of them die too. When many men attack, they make noise. The raiders run into the forest. Our men find an empty camp. Once, many years ago, the men of this village were ambushed. Ten of our families were left without husbands or fathers."

She rubbed her forehead, a habit she had when she was thinking deeply. "What will happen this time? What choices do we have? The men could attack the raiders' camp, but I told you what would happen then. Besides, Deep Lake, the War Chief, lies in the kiva unable to walk.

"The men could decide to stay here to guard the corn and the villages. Maybe the Navajos would attack and maybe they wouldn't. But by the time we knew, it would be too late for the buffalo hunt. And if the men go on the hunt anyway, we know the towns will be raided. It seems as if there is no good way out of this trap the Navajos have set for us."

"But Mother, we have to do *something!*"

"Yes, I know. But we must think first. Consider Quick Jay. If we attacked, they would kill him. And something else is very important. To interrupt the preparations for the dances might make the gods angry. We must find a better way." She pulled thoughtfully at her braids. "We can decide nothing now. You sleep. I will think about the matter."

Little Otter lay down and rolled up in his blanket.
His mother sat impassive, lost in thought. The firelight
flickered on her broad cheekbones and shone on her
black hair. She seemed to him to be as much a part of
the glow and the shadows as the cliffs and the mesas
were a part of the plateau.

Drowsily, he thought, I was sure she would go
straight to the kiva. Most women would. But my
mother is not like the others. Maybe that's why *I* feel
different too. Even if I were treated the same as the
other boys, I still wouldn't want to be just like them.
There are things I want to do that Gray Squirrel would
never dream of. Leaping Deer understood.

Suddenly he remembered something his godfather
had once said to him. It had been about that very
thing. He had asked Leaping Deer, "What is wrong
with wanting to be different?"

"Nothing," his godfather had replied, "if you choose
the right way of doing it. Think of the rain. When it
comes easy and gentle, it is good. But a cloudburst! The
fields are washed away, our crops are ruined, even the
birds and animals lose their homes."

"I understand that."

"And the snow. When it lies lightly on the mountains, it holds our water until we need it to help the
seeds burst their shells and grow. But blizzards are
killers of plants, woods creatures, even men."

Now, with his head buried in his blanket, Little Otter made a small grieving sound. His mother spoke
without turning.

"Go to sleep, my son. You are home now and all is
well."

Little Otter rolled over, and Leaping Deer's voice
sounded again as though he were sitting beside him.

"Most of us are content to be as much a part of our

village life as a raindrop is part of the pond into which it falls. But if you, Little Otter, must be different, let it be as the rain and the snow, not as the cloudburst or the blizzard. Be a builder, not a destroyer. Belong to the world. Don't hide from it. Remember these words, and someday you will understand what I mean."

But the villagers, Little Otter thought, won't let me alone to be either like them or different. I think perhaps they are afraid of those who don't belong.

He was just on the border of understanding, when his eyes closed in sleep.

BLUE CORN'S PLAN

The sun was showing a bright rim above the peaks when Blue Corn shook Little Otter awake. "Come! There is much to do today. Wake up."

Little Otter stretched, scratched and yawned. Then his eyes snapped open as he remembered. "The raiders! What about them?"

While he ate corn cakes, Blue Corn outlined her scheme. Little Otter grew more and more excited. "It ought to work, Mother! This plan sounds good. If we can get people to help, if everyone does his part well, if the rain gods help us, if . . ."

"There are too many ifs. But even so . . ."

"Whom will you ask to work with us?"

"Squash Blossom I can count on. I will speak to her first."

"But Mother, she's so slow!"

"Only when she has nothing to hurry for. Squash Blossom we *must* have, or there will be no others. But who else?"

"Snow Feather?"

"If you think he can keep the secret. He can tell his mother Squash Blossom needs his help."

"Quick Jay's mother?"

"Of course! The perfect one. No one could be more anxious. No one would work harder to make this a success. How worried she must be by this time!"

"And I? What should I do?"

"First get clay from the riverbank. The whitest you can find. And a bag of white powdery rock with the sparkling sand in it from the canyon to the north. Most important of all, be sure your coyote is in her den."

"Willow? Why?"

"I'll tell you later. She is a necessary part of the plan."

"She is?"

"Yes. Now no more questions. And not a word to anyone except Snow Feather. Be off with you!"

"I'll take Willow a few ears of green corn, and anything else that I find on the way. If she eats well this morning, she should sleep through the day. Is that all right?"

"I leave that to you. Don't go near the forest, though. You would not like to be a prisoner like Quick Jay. I go to Squash Blossom. If she agrees, we'll walk to the next village. There we can find Quick Jay's mother. She may be able to suggest others to help us."

The morning mists had burned away before mother and son met again at their doorway.

"There's to be a meeting at the village in the canyon," Blue Corn said after she had inspected Little Otter's packs of clay and sand. "We will hurry there. Did you ask Snow Feather?"

"Yes. He is very excited about it. I will go get him."

In the next village, they found a small gathering of carefully selected women and boys squatting on the floor of a cool, dim room. First Squash Blossom made a few remarks explaining the situation. Her wrinkled face was very solemn.

Little Otter looked around at the others. Shining Dew, Quick Jay's mother, was a strong, solid young woman whose eyes were swollen from crying. She walked nervously about, often striking one hand angrily with the other.

Over in the corner sat Shining Dew's sister and her son. In front squatted two of Quick Jay's older brothers and another cousin. Quick Jay's grandmother sat by the fire, stirring a pot of acrid-smelling dye. She grinned toothlessly at the newcomers.

Blue Corn, standing by the doorway, looked at the upturned faces. Would they accept her ideas? She was as much a foreigner to them as she was to her neighbors. Suppose they thought she was plotting with the raiders? She glanced uncertainly at Squash Blossom.

With a smile of encouragement, Pine Tip's aunt called Blue Corn to come stand beside her. "Blue Corn will now tell you our plan. It is a fine one. But it can work only if we all help. Listen carefully. You may think of some other ideas. All will be welcome."

Blue Corn drew a deep breath. So much depended upon the next few minutes. "You know why we are here," she said. "Also, we each know the importance of the buffalo dances, and how necessary they are for the hunt to be successful. Before I tell you our plan, though, I want to tell you something of the Navajos' beliefs. To know is to act more wisely when the time comes.

"A woman in our town across the mountains lived for many years among the Navajos. Many stories she told us. Night, of course, is the time when evil spirits roam. Everyone knows that. But the Navajos fear such beings far more than we do—especially witches and ghosts in enemy lands."

Her listeners nodded. That was understandable.

"Many creatures, they think, can be witches in disguise. Most of all, the owl, the wolf and the coyote. For the Navajos there are two paths in life. The white-pollen path is good. The yellow-pollen path is evil. To them, Coyote was the first animal on earth after First Man and First Woman arrived. Coyote could travel on both paths. But as time went on, he came to like the yellow one better. That is the path of mischief and destruction. So for them, a white coyote is good luck. But a yellow one is very bad luck."

Little Otter made a small sound. Blue Corn looked at him and smiled slightly before she continued.

"They tell many stories about Coyote. Most are about the terrible or funny things he did. A few are about the good things. The one we children asked for most was about First Man putting stars in the sky. He made a pattern of pebbles on the ground to show just how he wanted the sky to look at night. One by one, he carefully fastened the stars to the heavens to match his design of pebbles. First the unmoving star of the north and then the Seven Stars, those that look like a dipper, each put in exactly the right place.

"Coyote watched him. After a while he became impatient. First Man was so slow. Coyote said, 'You make a great hard task of an easy one. Here is the way.'

"With that, he grabbed up all the rest of the stars. He threw them into the air. They flew every which way, sticking to the sky wherever they happened to touch it. First Man was furious. All his fine plans were spoiled. But Coyote just laughed and went on his way. And the stars have stayed where he threw them from that day to this."

Blue Corn's listeners chuckled with delight. They loved a good story. And they forgot that Blue Corn was not one of them. Their doubts disappeared.

"Tonight," Blue Corn told them, "we will pretend to be witches and spirits."

"Witches?"

"Ghosts?"

"Yes. If we do it well, we will frighten the Navajos so much they will run away. They won't come back for a long time. Moon Old Man will help. Tonight he shows only a tiny slice of light. We hope the rain god and the cloud spirits will help too. A storm at the wrong time would be bad. It would wash the paint from our faces and bodies."

"Paint?"

"A great deal of it. Some of you will be owls. Others will howl like wolves. Most will be smeared with white clay. The Navajos believe witches and ghosts, if they are not in the shape of animals, to be white."

"But the raiders? What if they don't run?"

"That is a big chance," Blue Corn admitted. "We will carry knives, but will not use them unless it becomes absolutely necessary. Only if we are attacked. They are supposed to think we are spirits, so we should not get too close to them. They must not see us clearly or touch us. If they do, we are lost."

"Touch me? Ugh!"

One of the young cousins, Chipmunk, asked timidly, "What if *real* evil spirits come to get *us*?"

Little Otter gave him a scornful look, but Blue Corn answered gravely, "I have a stone to help, and I will make special charms to wear. But I fear the raiders more. They are terrible and cruel."

She looked around the group. "We are afraid. It is natural. But if anyone is too much afraid to help, say it now. On the mountain it will be too late. A mistake there, and we all die."

There was a long silence. People stared at the floor or the walls, avoiding one another's eyes. Blue Corn waited, her hands clenched. The wrong word would spoil everything.

Shining Dew broke the stillness. "I come with you. I say this is a good plan. Only one that is so different can save my little Quick Jay. Blue Corn, tell me what to do."

As the others echoed her words, Blue Corn knew she and Squash Blossom had won, at least so far. Even Quick Jay's grandmother rose stiffly to her feet. She came over to Blue Corn and said, "Blue Corn, I am an old woman. I cannot go. But I can care for the tiny one in the cradleboard for you while you are away."

Blue Corn nodded gratefully. "I will bring her over before we leave. It was a worry to me."

Soon they were all busy preparing horrible surprises for the unsuspecting raiders on the mountain.

During the hottest part of the day the ten plotters, each carrying a bundle, slipped quietly from their homes and met near Willow's den. Little Otter climbed to the cave and whistled for his pet. The coyote bounded out. She jumped up to lick his face. The others exclaimed in astonishment.

"A yellow coyote—as yellow as corn pollen!"

"It is tame!"

Snow Feather stared. "Little Otter, you didn't tell me. Oh, look at its ear! It's the same one, isn't it? How big it is now!"

Squash Blossom watched Willow, her head tilted. "Ummm . . . a golden coyote. And the Navajos think such ones to be witches. Ah, yes. My mother used to say that surprise can be a stronger weapon than the sharpest knife. Blue Corn, how can we fail?"

"In many ways, I fear. But we will do our best. Pray it is enough."

Little Otter led them up a deep canyon that cut through the plateau to the mountains. It was a long, hot climb. He was surprised to see that Squash Blossom, though she panted and sighed, easily kept up with the others.

"The excitement, I believe she likes it," he told Snow Feather, as his father's aunt held up her long skirt and climbed a steep bank, laughing when she slid back a few steps.

When they reached the head of the canyon, the sun was dropping toward the peaks. "We are not far from the raiders," Little Otter said. "The old hunting camp is just across that ridge to the north."

"Do any of you know of a hidden place?" Blue Corn asked. "A place where we can put on our paint and costumes? Where we can wait until dark?"

"Let me think." Squash Blossom sat on a big rock, puffed a bit and puckered her brow. The others rested and looked about them at the cliff walls and the winding trail. Willow, nose to the ground, poked into patches of scrub oak.

"Look!" Shining Dew pointed. "The mountain sheep! Up ahead."

"Beautiful!"

"How big his horns are!"

"What is that opening? There on the cliff below him?" Blue Corn asked.

"I had forgotten. How stupid this one is!" Squash Blossom clapped her hands to her cheeks. "It is the perfect place. An old cave used by the ancients. Very large."

"The trail to it, does it not join this one? I think I see where they come together."

In a few minutes, they were dropping their packs on the dry, dusty floor of the cave. Then they rested in the sunshine at the entrance. Some munched on pine nuts or corn cakes. Others were too tense and excited to eat.

Blue Corn said, "Little Otter, those cuts on Willow's shoulder. They are deep."

"That is where the eagle clawed her, Mother."

"Eagle! Clawed the coyote?" Snow Feather exclaimed. "Little Otter, you never tell me anything! Did you help your father catch the new chieftain-bird?"

"Everything has been so mixed up. It has happened so fast. But I'll tell you all about it when we get back."

"Will Willow let me look at her shoulder?" Blue Corn asked.

"If I am here."

Little Otter held Willow's head while his mother separated the golden hair to see if the wounds were healing. Her gentle fingers could find no sensitive spots or swelling along the scratches. Willow lifted her feet restlessly, but she endured the examination.

"It heals cleanly," Blue Corn finally said. She rubbed the coyote's head between the ears. "By herself she has kept out the dirt." She stood up. "A pretty animal. Well behaved. You have trained her well."

Chipmunk, watching nearby, came closer. "May I pet her?"

Before Little Otter could stop him, he reached out and patted Willow's back. The coyote whirled and snapped, and only Little Otter's equally quick tug at her neck fur prevented Chipmunk from having a badly bitten wrist.

"Don't! It upsets her. She's not used to people near. You had better stay away from her."

"Coyotes are coyotes, not dogs, little one," Blue Corn added kindly. "I wish, Little Otter, you had not kept her nearby. For your sake and for hers. But perhaps the gods knew we would need her tonight. It is foolish to question their wisdom. Now we must rest."

When the shadows darkened the canyon, Squash Blossom called them together. "We will put on our paint and costumes. But before that, we have a ceremony. Small and quiet, so that no one but the gods will hear."

From a small bag, Squash Blossom sprinkled corn-meal, sacred meal that would make a path to lead the gods to them. Then the women sat in a row along the side of the cave. They clapped their hands softly to the rhythm of the chant they sang, and the boys stamped back and forth, raising puffs of dust with their feet, in an ages-old dance they hoped would persuade the gods to deliver their enemies into their power. Even though it was done without the priest-chief or the elaborate headdresses or the long, careful preparations in the kivas, each one felt in his heart that the gods had heard and approved.

Then Blue Corn stood up briskly. "It is almost night."

"Will the storm come too early, do you think?" Shining Dew looked out anxiously at the dark clouds rising from behind the mountains. In the twilight, they were rimmed with pink and gold from the last glow of the setting sun.

"It is out of our hands."

Blue Corn began unpacking her bundle.

Because of the approaching storm, night came quickly. A chill breeze swept down the canyon. The boys shivered as they stood, dressed only in their breechclouts, while Blue Corn and Shining Dew smeared them with a paste of wet clay and sparkling white rock dust. Around their eyes and mouths the women made big black circles with the shiny black paint they used for their pottery decorations. When the job was finished, the boys looked at one another, grinning and teasing.

"You should see yourself," Snow Feather told Little Otter.

"I'm glad I can't!"

"Ho! How funny!" said another.

"It's not funny. We look awful!" Chipmunk said.

"What kind of creature are you?"

"I came out of a bad dream."

"Me too."

They made horrible faces and jumped around with their arms spread and their fingers curved like claws. Little Otter, painted like the rest, had an odd shaking in his stomach. He was glad he knew the others were only village boys. Chipmunk was right. They did look dreadful. He touched the little skin bag of charms his mother had tied about his neck. It made him feel better.

The women covered themselves with whatever they had been able to bring for the purpose. Squash Blossom donned an old bear-skin robe. Blue Corn fastened a rabbit-fur blanket about her shoulders. Shining Dew proudly displayed a worn wolf skin with the long, fluffy tail still attached. They painted their faces and hands white with clay and put on ugly demon headdresses they had made that morning from bits of animal skins, yucca fibers, paint, antlers, corncobs and feathers.

Blue Corn went from one to another—making suggestions, reminding them of their assigned roles and answering questions.

An hour after dark, they were ready. Then Blue Corn went off by herself to an open place on the trail. Squatting, she stared fixedly into a peculiarly shaped translucent object in her hand. It glowed faintly in the pale light that still washed the sky.

Little Otter followed her. "What is it, Mother? Why are you looking at that rock?"

She kept her eyes on the stone. "It's a special charm. My oldest brother gave it to me when I left. He said, 'To look in it is to see if witches or evil spirits are near.' "

Little Otter waited for several breaths. Then he whispered, "Are they?"

"No." She stood up. Her voice was strong and assured. "No, there are none. Come! We begin."

Joining the others, she said, "Little Otter will show us the way. You each know what to do. If all goes well, we meet here afterward. Do not linger. Do not stay in the clearing! We must be in and away again before they have time to think. Listen for the signals."

"What if they hear us coming?" Chipmunk asked.

"You mean, if they have sentries? I don't think they will. They know our men are in the kivas. Once we are near the camp, it will not matter. Then, the more noise the better."

Little Otter led them, breathless from the climb, up to a dense grove of trees. The ridge and the far rumble of thunder cut off the sound of their approach. After a few minutes' rest, they slipped noiselessly through the woods until they could see the glow of the campfire below them.

"It is time," Blue Corn murmured. "The gods go with us."

One by one, they disappeared into the darkness.

WITCHES
ON THE MOUNTAIN

The flames of the raiders' fire blew horizontal in the
angry gusts of wind that preceded the storm. Sparks
flew high, to lose themselves in the branches of the
swaying fir trees that creaked overhead. Little Otter,
huddled under the same tree that had sheltered him
the night before, reached out to touch Willow's warm
coat.

"Now," he whispered. "I give the signal!"

He opened his mouth, and from it came the long,
high yip-yipping howl of a coyote. It echoed over the
clearing below. Willow, puzzled to hear him make a
sound like that, stared with glowing yellow eyes. Then
she lifted her head and howled back. She sniffed, trot-
ting back and forth, and howled again.

The Navajos hunched their shoulders uneasily.
They watched the moving shadows of the forest. Then
they crouched closer to the fire, where a wild turkey
was roasting on a green stick. Little Otter could not
see the captive, Quick Jay. He must be in the hut, he
thought.

From a treetop drifted the eerie hoot of an owl. It

was made by one of the little captive's brothers. It sounded like a low, strangled moan. Then Little Otter heard roaring like that of the rain-bringer—the whirling device used during the rain dances to imitate thunder. Chipmunk had cleverly made an imitation and was swinging it around his head faster and faster. The roaring hum swelled and rebounded from the mountainsides until the little hollow was flooded with noise. It hurt Willow's sensitive ears, and she howled again and again.

The raiders jumped to their feet. Like terrified children, they looked at their leader. Crooked Nose tried to calm them, but other noises diverted their attention.

"Listen! Someone comes!"

"Your weapons! Get them!"

"I hear more than one."

"From that way."

"No, from down the hill."

"Stop arguing! You! Go see what makes that noise!"

Scar Chest reluctantly picked up a club and left the clearing. A moment later, the others heard a high scream. Scar Chest rushed into the firelight. His eyes bulged. The whites glistened like shiny shells.

"A bear! A bear with a devil's head!" He pointed with shaking finger.

"Fool! You're all fools. Frightened old women. I go myself."

With sullen, scared faces they watched Crooked Nose leave. Gathered close about the fire, they questioned Scar Chest. The wilderness seemed to reach for them with greedy arms. Suddenly one of them whirled as he heard a twig snap. He raised his bow and arrow. Then they fell from his nerveless hands. He made choking sounds as he backed away, followed by the others. There at the edge of the trees snarled a great wolf. It was as large as a human, but it had a white face and the head of a deer. Suddenly it disappeared.

"It's gone!"

"The great noise has stopped, too."

"Where did the wolf go?"

"The tree swallowed it."

"No, it flew up into the sky."

The forest came alive with sounds; the baying of a wolf; an owl's mournful hoots; a coyote's long, quavering song. The oak thickets crackled and shook. Tree branches bent and swayed unnaturally. Misshapen figures appeared and faded among the dark firs and white-trunked aspens. A real owl, disturbed by the racket, left its hole in a dead tree and flew low over the fire with a heavy, soft flapping of great wings. The Navajos ducked and covered their heads with their arms.

"Look out!"

"It is bad luck!"

"A ghost!"

They jerked around as Crooked Nose almost fell into the clearing. "I saw a *thing*!" he gasped. "With fur. A bear, I thought. I raised the club. Then you wouldn't believe it. A spirit in a tree pulled the club out of my hand and hit me with it! The bear turned around. It had a big yellow head. It was a witch!"

The others wailed loudly. They raised their arms, begging their gods for protection. A shriek of maniacal laughter now made Little Otter's skin crawl, even though he had been expecting it. The raiders cowered together. Across the open space beyond the fire they saw two white, wild creatures capering in a weird dance. In the glimmer of the flames, the small bodies glittered and sparkled like snow in the sunset.

Three of the Navajos broke from the circle. Rushing

up the mountain, they passed near Little Otter's hiding place. Willow bounded after them. They heard her coming. Looking back, they saw her silhouetted against the glow of the fire.

"A witch!"

"Run! Faster!"

"It is on us!"

They blundered against trees and stumbled over fallen branches. Little Otter's grin changed to delighted laughter as Willow leaped against the legs of one of the men, knocking him down. It seemed a shame to spoil the fun, but he needed Willow with him. He blew on his bone whistle. In a few moments Willow rejoined him, her tongue lolling out. She nudged his arm. Little Otter choked down another laugh. She acted so satisfied with herself.

Down in the clearing, Scar Chest threw an armload of wood on the fire. It blazed up. But it only made the shadows seem darker than before. The remaining raiders hesitated, shaken with fear. They were torn between an overwhelming desire to flee and terror of the unknown forest where so many evil spirits roamed. Overhead, the clouds closed in. Thunder rolled and rumbled. Lightning flared, blinding in its sudden glare and the blackness that followed.

This is going to be a big storm, Little Otter thought. His scalp prickled with the electricity in the air.

Then, in an instant, the skies cracked open. Thunder boomed. At the same moment, a lightning bolt struck a pine farther up the mountain. The great tree split and fell, breaking other trees in its path as it crashed to earth.

The air quivered. Little Otter grabbed Willow. His ears were ringing. He smelled the pungent tang of charred wood. The hush that followed was utter, com-

plete, as though the world itself were stunned to silence. Then a gust, and the branches over his head stirred. Through the stillness, he heard the sudden, surging roar of the approaching wind and rain.

Little Otter shook his head to clear it. "Our turn, Willow. Hurry, before it's too late!"

He crawled out from under the tree. His eerie shriek rose and fell until it gurgled away in a long, wailing groan. Then he jumped down into the clearing. Willow followed right behind him. Howling and waving his arms, the painted boy ran straight at the men huddled by the fire. Almost upon them, he swerved out into the darkness. Willow leaped and snarled beside him.

Again Little Otter crossed the clearing. This time he yowled and spat like an angry bobcat. Clawing toward their throats, he passed so close to the Navajos that he smelled the sweat of fear on their bodies. They tripped over one another as they fell away from him. One stumbled into the fire. He yelled, brushing off the burning coals.

"He pushed me! Did you see? The witch pushed me!"

Little Otter, safe in the woods, gasped for air. He hadn't realized he had been holding his breath. But this time Willow was not beside him. She had paused in the clearing. The odor of the cooking turkey, forgotten but still spitted over the fire, was too much for her. She jumped. Little Otter stifled a hysterical giggle. Spit and turkey were now clamped between the coyote's jaws. Triumphantly, she bore her prize off into the forest.

The raiders erupted into action as though the mountain had exploded beneath their feet.

"Witches!"

"A yellow coyote!"

"It's a warning! Run!"

"A ghost and a witch!"

One man began to shake and moan crazily. Crooked Nose lashed out with his fist. The moaning stopped, but the raider lay on the ground, rolling and jerking. The other men darted about, bumping into one another.

"Get out of my way!"

"It's haunted here."

"This way."

"No! The trail is over there."

"Hurry, before the yellow witch comes back!"

"If we can only get home safely . . ."

"Never will I come here again!"

"Let's go!"

"Run!"

Finding the path at last, they raced up toward the round valley among the peaks. Even the one who had been groveling on the ground jumped up and ran with the others. They stopped for nothing. All their gear, their weapons were left behind. And around the clearing, many black-ringed eyes in white-painted faces watched them go.

Little Otter waited for a moment. Then he leaped past the campfire and ducked into the small hut. In a corner, Quick Jay pressed himself against the wall in the darkness.

"Go away, ghost," he quavered.

"Silly! I'm no ghost. Come on, your mother is here. The Navajos have gone."

Little Otter grabbed the child and half-carried, half-pulled him outside. Eager arms lifted the little boy released from captivity. He celebrated his freedom by weeping loudly. Shining Dew put her face close to his.

"Quick Jay! It is I, your mother!" The sobbing increased in volume. She spoke louder. "Listen to me, my son. This is a costume, as for a dance. See? Does not your mother look funny?"

At last Quick Jay heard the words. He leaned back and recognized his mother beneath the paint and fur. His crying turned to relieved, exhausted laughter. It was hard for him to believe the nightmare was over.

Squash Blossom poked her head around a bush and then came out into the clearing. "There you are!" she said to Snow Feather. "This old one thanks you. How quickly you acted! Taking that club away from the crooked-nosed one when he would have struck me. You were very brave. Otherwise I would be dead. And maybe the others too."

Snow Feather sat down as though his knees were water. "I didn't stop to think. Now I'm scared. He was right under my tree. When he lifted his arm, I just leaned out and grabbed the club and hit him with it. I did it without thinking."

"A good thing! But we must leave here. Tell the others. The fire is too bright."

The thunder god spoke again, and the wind roared through the trees. From the edge of the aspen grove, Blue Corn beckoned Little Otter to her side. She had to put her mouth close to his ear to be heard.

"Follow the raiders, you and Willow! Be sure they really start across the mountains. If necessary, hurry them on their way. Then meet us in the cave. We'll build a fire there and wait until the storm passes."

"It worked, Mother! Your plan worked. The villages are safe."

"I think so. With the gods' blessings. Now, run! The storm is upon us."

"Who cares now? We have won!"

By midmorning of the next day, every person in both villages had heard again and again how the raiders had been frightened away. There was rejoicing and singing in the town squares. In the kivas, the men received the exciting news from the women who brought their food.

It rained again that afternoon and also in the evening. Already the earth was showing a haze of green. The corn and squash were growing so fast that Little Otter was sure he could see the vines and stalks move.

Blue Corn shrugged off her sudden fame. Quietly she went about her usual tasks. She knew there were probably as many hidden resentments as there were genuine changes of heart. And so she was truly surprised when several of the women, headed by her neighbor Brown Bird, came to visit. Shyly they offered gifts of cactus fruit, a freshly skinned rabbit, a handful of pine nuts. She welcomed them graciously, putting food before them in her most beautiful bowls. All of them acted as though there were nothing unusual about the occasion. To have behaved otherwise would have shown bad manners.

Before they rose to leave, Brown Bird touched one of the dishes. "Would you . . . do you think . . . ?" She bent her head bashfully. "Your designs, they fit the bowls so well. I try. They do not come out like yours, so neat. Would you show me how?"

"Our feather design," said another. "It looks well on water jugs. Why do you not use it sometimes?"

And a third added, "Working together is pleasant. The time goes quickly. We miss your presence, Blue Corn."

"Yes. Please, join us. Tomorrow we make pots. Come work with us."

Blue Corn looked from one embarrassed face to another. She hesitated. Then she smiled. "I would be happy to come. And to use the feather design. You will teach it to me?"

"That, and many others," Brown Bird said, as the women filed out.

After her visitors had gone, Blue Corn turned around. Little Otter was amazed to see her wipe a tear from the corner of her eye. She really cares, he thought, cares what they think of her. She has always held her head so proudly, I didn't know.

"Why were you so nice to them?" he demanded. "After the way they have treated you—after these long years?"

"It *has* been long, too long. I do not forget that. Almost I answered them proudly, angrily. But what if I had? For a moment I would have had satisfaction. And for years ahead this one would still be shunned, lonely. To feed my pride is not worth the price. Consider, too, that coming here was not easy for them, either."

"I guess so. You are right, my mother. It will be better now."

Blue Corn's lips trembled slightly. "It is no small victory, Little Otter. They have made me one of them. How wonderful to no longer be a stranger in their land! Now it is my land too."

She picked up her finest water jar and balanced it on her head with joyous grace. "I return soon." She began to sing softly, and the notes hung sweetly in the air after she had gone.

When it came to talking about his own role in scaring away the raiders, Little Otter followed his mother's example. But he eagerly told all who would listen about the golden coyote, his wonderful Willow. When he went to her den, however, she was still sleeping, and he tiptoed away without disturbing her. The rest of the afternoon he spent with Snow Feather, telling him the whole story from the beginning.

LiTTLE OTTER'S JOURNEY

By the next day, the day of the buffalo dances, the villages had returned to normal. Dawn was faintly tinting the sky when a messenger, Arrow, who was Gray Squirrel's father, called from outside the doorway of Pine Tip's home. Blue Corn shook Little Otter awake. He stumbled out to his visitor. Rubbing his eyes sleepily, he almost forgot to give the proper greeting.

Arrow laughed. "Your father desires to speak with you in the kiva at once. The dances begin soon. Otherwise this one would not have waked you before the sun. Come! I take you to him."

As they walked across the square and out around the community houses, Little Otter wondered what his father wanted. Would Willow now be allowed to stay? His heart beat faster at the thought. Then a shout from behind them brought them to a halt.

"Wait! Little Otter!" It was Chipmunk, from the other village. He ran as he called.

"To talk is necessary. I was just coming to see you."

Arrow nodded his permission. "But only for a moment."

Little Otter went to meet Chipmunk, who said

breathlessly, "I was watching the fields when it happened. It was a little while ago. I had to come right away. You'll know what to do."

He looked around and leaned closer. "Your coyote came up on our mesa. She came to the fields. It was early, still almost dark."

"Are you sure? Willow?"

"There was enough light to see her golden coat, and the ear with the piece missing. I let her steal some corn. After all, who deserves it more? But when she had enough, when I tried to chase her away, she ran at me! I remembered the other evening, how she snapped, and I turned my back and covered my face. I was scared! But that Willow! She knocked me over, and stood over me. Almost it seemed she laughed. Then she just ran away. She didn't hurt me at all."

Little Otter bit his lip. "I *told* her . . ."

"I would have said nothing, but for the rest."

"There's more?"

"Yes. When I went down to the village, I passed our turkey pens. There were coyote tracks there too. I rubbed them out. No one else saw them. But I had to tell you. Should I have done something else?"

"No, Chipmunk, you did the right thing. Thank you for coming. I'll . . ." He sighed and spread his hands helplessly. "Don't worry. She won't do it again. I'll see to that. I'll find some way." But for all his brave words, Little Otter's face was troubled as he rejoined Arrow and went with him to the kiva.

Pine Tip was waiting at the foot of the long ladder. He led his son past the men who were working on costumes and prayer sticks. In a quiet corner near the altar, they squatted on the floor.

"The raiders. We heard the story. How proud I am of you! And of your mother! You were very courageous and imaginative. When Red Hawk was told, he called the others together. They have decided. You may go on the buffalo hunt after all. I'm glad for you, and for myself too. To tell you now is to give you time to prepare for the journey."

Touching Little Otter's shoulder, he added. "One thing more. Your coyote. There is no person in either village who will harm her now. She came willingly. She answered our need. Should she get into more mischief, she is safe from us. The decision as to what to do with her is yours. It is out of my hands. Do you understand?"

Little Otter nodded soberly. After a moment he said, "The buffalo hunt." Thoughtfully he pulled at one earlobe. "I wanted to go so badly. More than anything I wanted to go. Now . . . Oh, Father, may I think about it and tell you tonight after the dances are over?"

"Of course."

As they started toward the ladder, Gray Squirrel crossed the room to meet them. He spoke stiffly.

"Little Otter, there is something I must say. I'm sorry about teasing and pestering you. It was wrong. And what I said about you and your mother . . . well, we're lucky to have you here in our village. I was silly and mean. I'm sorry. I'll really try to do better."

Then he glanced over to where his father was watching sternly. He flushed. Pushing his hair back from his face, he said with a grin, "He told me to apologize. But I would have done it anyway. Truly. Will you be friends with this stupid one?"

Little Otter opened his mouth for a sharp retort. Then he thought of his mother. Only a moment's satisfaction, she had said.

Instead he smiled. "Gladly."

Gray Squirrel turned and took a few steps. Then he came back. "Ah . . . I want to ask you something."

"What?"

"Well, I know now the coyote is a tame one. But the other day up on the mesa. Can you tell me how you got away?"

Little Otter's eyes sparkled with laughter. "There's an old trail on the other side. I hid in a cave. Sometime I'll show you."

"Oh, so that was it! I feel better. For a while I wondered, maybe you really *could* fly. On the hunt we can talk. You'll come, of course? You can teach me things I don't know, things like how to make friends. I guess I go about it all wrong. But I want to learn."

"I would like to go, but I'm not sure yet."

"I hope you do."

"There is something else I had thought of doing, but . . . I'll have to think. Thank you, anyway."

As Pine Tip and Little Otter passed, those on either side nodded or smiled or made joking remarks. Their approval warmed Little Otter inside. He told his father goodbye at the foot of the ladder.

As he mounted the smooth, worn rungs, the boy thought the climb from the firelight in the kiva to the dawn outside was the longest one he had ever made. Would he ever know where he really belonged?

There were so many thoughts going through his head, so many decisions to make. The buffalo hunt, his plan to run away, Willow.

I wish Leaping Deer were here, he thought. He would help me. He would tell me what to do.

In a few words he told Blue Corn what had been said in the kiva. "I must think . . . make up my mind. I'll go to Willow. Before the dances begin, I'll be back."

When he crossed the square, he looked back. His mother was still standing in the doorway. Her smile was happy—and yet a little sad too, he thought. What was she thinking? Did she suspect that he wanted to go to her home village? He didn't know.

A short time later, he and Willow lay atop the rock above the place where he had found her. So much had happened since that hot summer day. Willow herself had grown from scrawny pup to beautiful maturity. He stroked her gently. She nuzzled him with her long nose. The black tip of her tail twitched back and forth.

Little Otter rubbed his arms to warm them. The sun had not yet arrived to disperse the early-morning chill. He gazed out over the great valley to the high blue peaks of the eastern mountains. He had so much to decide, for Willow as well as for himself. And there was no one to help him. He looked around. He was alone except for Willow. And, oh yes, the mountain sheep. It was standing on Signal Rock, the highest point on the mesa to the west. As he watched, the great sheep turned. With strong, graceful leaps, it disappeared behind a crag. It was gone. Now he was really alone. Even Willow had gone roaming off across the rocks. It was a scary feeling. Deciding things for himself was not as simple or as much fun as he had thought it would be.

Only when he saw people gathering in the square across the canyon did he leave his high perch and slowly make his way down the steep trail in the cliff. Willow, who had returned to his side, left him then, loping off toward her den, where she would sleep until she woke to hunt later in the afternoon.

The sun god arose. The sky turned pink. As the red rim appeared above the mountain peaks, the buffalo dances began. They continued all day. As the men filed into and out of the kivas or stamped and chanted in the square, Little Otter took special pride in the white eagle feathers waving from the prayer sticks and bobbing up and down on the costumes of the dancers. Surely the chieftain-bird's plumage would speed the prayers of the people to the gods, who could not fail to hear and be pleased.

It was dusk when the dances were over. The men scattered to their homes to make their final preparations to leave at dawn. Pine Tip stood in his doorway and looked about the room.

"Little Otter! The journey! You have nothing ready. I don't understand."

"I have decided not to go, Father."

"But . . ."

"There will be many hunts in years to come. But now I want to . . . I mean . . . Father, I must do something else."

"Oh?" Pine Tip was taken aback. He was also disappointed. Then he smiled and gripped his son's arm with strong fingers. "But next year, next year we go together! Still, I must admit that to have you here is to worry less about your mother and little Shell Flower. You will take good care of them."

Little Otter didn't answer. His throat was too full.

That night he rolled and muttered in his sleep. When he awoke at dawn, he was still tired. Standing with the others who were staying behind, he waved farewell as the hunters shouldered their bundles and took the trail to the eastern mountains and to the buffalo plains on the other side. He walked to the edge of the mesa. There he watched until the long line of men far below had snaked its way between the high cliffs and rounded a bend in the canyon. They were gone.

Afterward he walked slowly back to the community house to get his things together, the necessary items he had taken when he had started out just three days before to go to his mother's village on the other side of the range. He still had his own journey to make.

Two days later, he stood on the far slope of the round valley in the western mountains. Through the meadow below him ran the small river that could lead him to the villages of his mother's people. Willow crouched beside him, her head raised, ears cocked. She sniffed the air and scratched restlessly. Little Otter petted her, fondling the ear with the notch in it.

The night before, as they warmed themselves by a small fire, they had heard the evening singing of other coyotes, and once they had seen one silhouetted against the tip-tilted moon, a crescent that looked to Little Otter like a bright bowl spilling a path of shining corn pollen across the heavens. He remembered the story of Coyote and the stars, and laughed aloud. Willow, he thought fondly, lived up to her first ancestor. She too was a prankster.

Last night, though, with songs of her own kind echoing around her, Willow had not been interested in tricks. Instead, she had paced nervously about. Sometimes she had answered the calls with her own wavering, high song. I would know her voice anywhere, Little Otter thought.

Now, in the morning coolness, she sat beside him looking over the new country, searching for a glimpse of the coyotes she had heard in the night. Suddenly she jumped up and stood tense, expectant. Two does with fawns filed slowly from the shelter of the trees. They hesitated, listened with great ears, then stepped delicately across the meadow to drink at the stream.

Willow only glanced at the deer. Then her gaze returned to the fringe of the forest. Little Otter smiled

when he saw what she was staring at so intently. Another coyote stood in the shadows.

The boy was more interested in the deer. He was hungry for venison. He reached for his bow and arrows. Then he shrugged. He was too far from the does to hit one of them, and he didn't want to take the time to stalk them until he was close enough for a good shot. So he too only watched.

One of the deer lifted her head. She scanned the surrounding countryside, her large ears cupped to catch any sound. She started as Little Otter slapped at a gnat. Alarmed, she bounded off, followed by the others. Their white rumps flashed against the green of grass and trees. The coyote in the shadows emerged and trotted after them. Willow shifted, her muscles rippling under her bright coat.

Little Otter touched her head tenderly. "All right. Go along, my Willow. Join the other coyotes. That's where you belong. Go on!"

She nuzzled his hand. He thought he saw regret in her slanted golden eyes.

"Go!" he repeated, and stepped away from her side.

She trotted forward, then paused and stared back at him. He picked up a pinecone and tossed it. It missed her, perhaps because his eyes were blurred with tears. She stood, one foreleg lifted. The boy held his breath. Then Willow made a soft, whining sound in her throat, loped off across the grassy slope and leaped the stream. On the other side she halted again, looked at him for a long moment, then turned and entered the forest.

Little Otter watched her go, her back glinting in the bright rays of the swiftly rising sun. Sniffing, he drew in a ragged breath that sounded like a sob. He brushed his hand across his eyes. When he took it away, it was wet. With a sigh, he picked up his pack and slowly started back toward his own village on the mesa.

There was a new pride on his face, a new sureness in his step. For all his sadness, he was happy, too. He was doing what he knew Leaping Deer would have wanted him to do.

But it's more than that, he thought. Now I know where I belong too. At last, I know.

Yet a wisdom born of love told him he would never again be the same. Something wild and young and free, something eternally golden, had departed from his heart to roam the ranges, to run forever with the golden coyote.

POSTSCRIPT

This is, of course, an imaginary story. As far as I know, there never was a boy named Little Otter who had a tame coyote called Willow. But there *was* a village on the mesa, and it was probably much as I have described it. It is now called Tsankawi, which means "ruins on the mesa above the gap of the sharp, round cactus." It is a part of Bandelier National Monument, on the Pajarito Plateau in New Mexico. The Tewas of San Ildefonso Pueblo claim it as one of their ancestral homes.

Here one may see the fallen walls of the great community buildings, the roofless pits of the kivas, the paths worn deep in the soft volcanic stone by the bare feet of laughing brown children and the sandals of their parents during the period of several centuries when the village was occupied. Petroglyphs—carvings of birds and animals and dancing gods—decorate the cliffs and the interiors of smoke-blackened caves.

Shattered bits of pottery—called sherds—are everywhere. Sometimes the fragments show the fingerprints of the women who formed and smoothed and painted the bowls and jars so long ago. Myriad chips of obsidian and quartz, basalt and agate tell of a time when tools and weapons were of stone and bone and wood, objects made by the men who used them.

Modern children climb from ground to ledge and path to mesa top using hand-and-toeholds carved into rock walls by gallant, tenacious, peaceful people long before the Pilgrims landed in New England.

Within a century or two after the events of this book might have taken place, and after the Indians had moved their pueblos to the valley of the Rio Grande, these early Americans were overwhelmed by the Spanish Conquistadores—first by the soldiers of Coronado in 1540, and then by the colonizing forces of Don Juan de Oñate in 1598. To ensure their own survival, the Indians made certain concessions to their conquerors. But their quiet life patterns of harmony and reason persisted within the pueblos. Their stubborn strength prevails even now in adobe villages centered about dance squares and ancient kivas in northern New Mexico and Arizona.

Today the sun still stains the jagged peaks of the Sangre de Cristos a deep rose-red as it slowly dips behind the dark, humped mountains of the Jemez range to the west. The Tewas—descendents of the people of Tsankawi and its sister pueblo, Otowi, the village in the canyon—live in the valley below the plateau. Many of their songs and dances are those performed by their ancestors before the Spanish came. One of them is the Buffalo Dance. At special times, present-day Tewas may return to sacred shrines on the mesas for quiet ceremonies that have been passed down from generation to generation for longer than any of them can know for sure.

Today, as then, deer, elk, bears, cougars and other wild creatures roam the dense evergreen forests on the mountain slopes and drink from cold, tumbling streams in deep canyons. The grass grows lush in the Valle Grande, the great round valley among the Jemez peaks, and trout jump in the little river that leads to the pueblos on the western side of the mountains.

Often on a summer night one may hear a coyote sing to the moon from the ruins on the mesa. Whether or not it has a golden coat I cannot say.

EILEEN THOMPSON

Los Alamos, New Mexico